Clara Sophia Bloomfield-Moore

Gondaline's lesson: The warden's tale

Stories for children and other poems

Clara Sophia Bloomfield-Moore

Gondaline's lesson: The warden's tale
Stories for children and other poems

ISBN/EAN: 9783337137687

Printed in Europe, USA, Canada, Australia, Japan

Cover: Foto ©Andreas Hilbeck / pixelio.de

More available books at **www.hansebooks.com**

GONDALINE'S LESSON

AND OTHER POEMS

GONDALINE'S LESSON

THE WARDEN'S TALE

STORIES FOR CHILDREN

AND OTHER POEMS

BY

MRS BLOOMFIELD MOORE

'Disdain us not, O kindly heart of man !
Us unregarded poets of the earth,
The feeble songsters singing as we can
Our eager melodies of little worth'

LONDON

C. KEGAN PAUL & CO., 1 PATERNOSTER SQUARE

1881

Dedicated

ONE WHO HAS 'GONE BEFORE'

' Ever near us, though unseen,
  The dear immortal spirits tread ;
For all the boundless universe
  Is life—there are no dead '

CONTENTS.

—◆—

MISCELLANEOUS.

	PAGE
GONDALINE'S LESSON	3
LOVE'S FOUR SEASONS	8
THE WARDEN'S TALE	11
THE WEB OF LIFE	18
THE MAIDEN'S FLOWER OMENS	19
BLOSSOMS AND THORNS	23
THE MAGDALENE	25
CHAFF AND WHEAT	29
LOVE AND FAME	30
THE SOUL'S CITADEL	36
THE STORY OF MY LOVE	38
THE CUP OF LIFE	40
REAL AND IDEAL	42
WORDS	44
DRIFTED AWAY	45
RESIGNATION	47
THE ARMOUR OF LOVE	49
PEACE THAT PASSETH UNDERSTANDING	51
THE STRANGER	52
A PICTURE	54
'WOULD I WERE AT REST'	56
LEAVING STOCKHOLM, MARCH 1874	58
MIDWAY	60

a

	PAGE
TO ONE WHO DISLIKES FLOWERS	62
DESERTED	64
A VALENTINE	66
IN EGYPT	68
TO A STUDENT	70
MY HEART	72
ANTICIPATION	74
BETRAYED	76
A GIFT OF FLOWERS	79
THE FAITHLESS LOVER	81
THE ENTHUSIAST	83
SONG OF THE FORSAKEN	85
THE APPROACH	87
ANSWER TO THE HYMN	88
LETTERS	91
IT MIGHT HAVE BEEN	92
GRIEF, CONSCIENCE, AND FAITH	93
THE COUNTRY	95
HOME	98
GRAND-CHILDREN	100
MAUD	102
THE MESSAGE	104
COMPENSATION	106
SYMPATHY	108
HOW LONG?	109
A MEMORY OF THE NILE	110
GENESEE FALLS	114
NIAGARA BELOW THE CATARACT	115

CONTENTS.

	PAGE
THE BROKEN TRYST	116
THE DYING WIFE	118
INVOCATION	121

IN MEMORIAM.

THE MIDNIGHT VIGIL	125
AFTER THE VIGIL	127
DEATH	129
ISABEL	131
MEMORIES	133
A DIRGE	135
AN ANNIVERSARY	137
A TRIBUTE	139
AN AUTUMN SUNSET	141
A PSALM OF THANKSGIVING	143
'BABY ERNALD'	144
'NOT LOST, BUT GONE BEFORE'	145

STORIES FOR CHILDREN.

'KATIE DID:' A GOSSIP'S TALE	153
COWARDS	159
DOGGEREL	161
THE BIRDS' NEST	163
THE LITTLE TRUANT	166

VOICES OF THE PAST.

MY COUNTRY	171
'FORWARD, MARCH'	173
IN ROME, MAY 1863	175

x CONTENTS.

PAGE

AT HOME, MAY 1864 .   177

WIDOWED 178

OUR HERO 181

THE SEASONS.

AN APRIL DAY . .   185

A DAY IN MIDSUMMER . . 187

AUTUMN SCENES 190

WINTER 192

SONNETS.

I. MORNING 197

II. NOON 198

III. NIGHT 199

ERAS IN LIFE.

FOREBODINGS . . 203

THORNS AND ARROWS 204

MY GETHSEMANE 207

'O GOD, BE PITIFUL' 209

'BE BRAVE' 211

SUBMISSION 212

EVIL AND GOOD 214

WRECKED 216

DEAD HOPES . . 218

WAITING 220

MEMORIAL 222

THE MINISTERING SPIRIT . . . 224

MISCELLANEOUS.

B

POEMS.

GONDALINE'S LESSON.

Faust.—Nun gut, wer bist du denn?
Meph.—Ein Theil von jener Kraft die stets das Böse will, und stets das Gute schafft.—GOETHE.

[*Faust.*—Well, good! who art thou then?
Meph.—A part of that power that always wants evil, but always creates good.]

THE Prince of Evil from his lurid home
　　Sent to our world, on mission fraught with ill,
An angel wondrous fair to look upon,
　　A Lucifer in point of cunning skill.

Landing on earth, the angel walked with men ;
　　They knew him not as other than their kin:
And one, ruling as lord in wide domain,
　　Threw open doors and took the angel in.

With form like Juno's and a heart of gold,
　　Fairer than Helen, was his beauteous queen :
Gracious as goddess stooping down to man
　　The stranger guest was met by Gondaline.

The angel held aloof, nor sought to win
　　One smile other than those she freely gave ;
Serene his front as theirs who never sin,
　　Serene his eyes as theirs who live to save.

The days passed on, and like a sister kind
　　Grew day by day the fair and gracious queen ;
The weeks passed by, and like a sister fond
　　More gracious grew the lovely Gondaline.

When one full month had folded happy days,
　　As the ripe wheat folds close within its core
The hoarded sweetness of the sun's warm rays
　　When drooping sheaves are bound for garnered
　　store,

The angel guest feigned that he must depart—
　　Deep sadness in his eyes and in his mien,
Trembled his voice whene'er he spoke unto
　　The trustful, gentle, gracious Gondaline.

'Why wilt thou leave us?' the fair woman asked,
　　And none were near to hear the answer given.
'I go,' he said, 'because I dare not stay :
　　I am as one shut out from hopes of heaven.'

'And why is this?'   Her eyes were raised to his.
  'Some secret meaning in your words are hid.'
'You say aright : I dare not plainer speak
  Unless by your sweet lips mine own are bid.'

'Tell me thy grief,' she said, 'and I will pray
  Unto our Lord to lift the heavy load.'
He shuddered as she spoke, and turned away
  As one who finds a barrier on his road.

'Fear not.   I will thy secret guard
  As if it were a secret of my own.
I would that I could help thee on thy way—
  Burdens are lightened when not borne alone.'

'Ah, thou couldst help me if thou wouldst,' he said ;
  'But in dark ways thy feet have never trod,
And thou wouldst fear to go where I must walk !'
  'Nothing I fear save conscience and my God !'

Again he quailed and cowered at the word ;
  Then raised his eyes, and met her questioning
    gaze :
Hers were as virginal as maiden's are ;
  His with dark passions were ablaze.

' I am no coward,' said she unto him,
　' And in those ways, howe'er so dark they be,
I should not fear, nor from them turn aside,
　If in them I could be of use to thee.'

Nearer she drew, and took his hand in hers,
　Nor did she fear when close he held her own ;
Nearer he drew, and bent his face to hers,
　Saying some words in low and eager tone.

She felt his gaze as snow feels morning sun,
　While her lips moved in earnest, pleading prayer :
' Dear Lord, give me this precious soul to save !
　Help him, whate'er it is, his cross to bear !'

Once more he shrank, as if a thing of naught ;
　Once more their eyes were turned in steadfast
　　gaze :
It was as if some power passed from her,
　Drawing him from the evil of his ways.

' I would not harm thee if I could,' he said :
　' I go to tell my master I have seen
A spirit pure as heaven's angels are,
　In thy chaste eyes, thou wondrous Gondaline.

' I go to tell him that I cannot fill

The harmful mission which his mandate sent :

I would not wrong thee, if I could,' he said,

While on him still her questioning eyes were bent.

' How couldst thou wrong me ?' she the answer
made.

'I seek to do thee good; thou couldst not do me
ill !

All things together work for weal, we know,

To those who work for good and seek God's will.

' Thy master hath no power, save God permits ;

And He guards those who strive to do His will :

Go, tell thy master this, whose evil good may bring

To thee, and me, God's purpose to fulfil.

' I know thee now—a minister of Sin !

But thou a lesson unto me hast taught :

The soul of good may e'en in evil dwell,

The soul of evil e'en in good be brought !'

LOVE'S FOUR SEASONS.

'Where love is, heaven is.'
BARBARA'S HISTORY.

I

WHAT time sad Winter's snows cold-sowed the
earth,
And leaden skies hid heaven from our sight,
While wrangling winds wailed o'er their tortured
birth
Through short cold days and long cold hours of
night,
Love planted in my heart his seeds of fire,
Thrilling each vein with vibrant, strange delight,
Changing my pulses to electric wire,
Though still his face was hidden from my sight.

II

What time the goddess of the Spring came down
To bring her yearly offering of flowers,
And Earth threw off her icy veil and gown,
Her bosom quickening in the sun-god's showers,

When virginal fields of pale forget-me-not
Couched side by side with amorous clover lay,
Then walked I in those fields with Love, I wot,
Still blindly trusting him to lead the way.

III

What time hot Summer's throbbing skies of blue
Shone o'er these meadows where our steps had
strayed,
And her warm breath, steeped in rich fragrance
through,
Filled with sweet languors all the hours we
made,
I saw Love's face, and all my blood to flame
He kindled with his asking eyes on mine ;
And I, divining what he wished to claim,
Said in my heart, 'Already I am thine.'

IV

What time the purple grapes hung on the vine,
And pregnant Earth was teeming with her fruit,
And men and maidens harvested the wine,
Dancing at close to zittern and to lute :

Within Love's arms, close circling me around,
   Languid with kisses which his warm lips rained,
I said, 'At last life's secret I have found,
   At last my earthly paradise is gained.'

'

THE WARDEN'S TALE.

A PARABLE FOR THE AGE.

Oh, the little more, and how much it is,
And the little less, and what worlds away.
R. BROWNING.

I

I AM warden of a garden—
Of a garden quaint and fair—
Seldom does the king, my master,
 Ever wish to wander there.

II

Little cares he for the blossoms
 Or the fruits beside the wall;
In the centre blooms a rose tree,
 And the roses he claims all.

III

But one day there came a pilgrim,
 Lofty air yet winning mien,
And he asked a tiny flower
 Pale as is the moonlight's sheen.

IV

So I plucked and gave it to him,
  And he wore it on his breast
As we walked along the garden,
  Pausing here and there to rest.

V

Day by day returned this pilgrim;
  As we paced the shaded aisles
Friendlier grew his words of greeting,
  Tenderer his friendly smiles.

VI

And we often gathered flowers—
  Spotless lilies, pansies cold
As the purple in the heavens
  When it borders twilight's gold.

VII

But one day our footsteps straying
  To the garden's centre came,
Where the roses on the branches
  Bloomed with tropic hearts of flame.

VIII

Then with lips so sweet and tender,
　And with eyes more tender still,
'Give me but one rose,' he whispered,
　'And then ask whate'er you will.'

IX

How could I the rose refuse him,
　If his eyes my heart could melt?
So I stretched my hand to reach it,
　When a piercing thorn I felt.

X

'Ah! 'tis not my rose to give you!'
　With an aching heart I spake,
In the pain of that refusing
　Which I longed to have him take.

XI

''Tis but one rose that I asked for,'
　Straight he said, in grieved surprise;
'When your master counts so many,
　Bloom they only for his eyes?'

XII

'Take the violets, take the pansies,
　　Take the lilies, if you will,
But unworthy I for warden
　　If no trust I shall fulfil.

XIII

'And this rose bush, he has told me,
　　Must be left for him alone ;
So I cannot give his roses,
　　Though they are so thickly blown.'

XIV

'Give me one ; he will not miss it
　　Though he count them o'er and o'er—
Only one ; 'tis all I ask for,
　　And I ne'er will ask for more.

XV

'Give it, warden ; lips refusing
　　Wear not grace as when they yield ;
And I know the king, thy master,
　　Gathers in another field.'

XVI

Then I wavered. In that moment
He knew not the half my pain
As I answered, ' Reach and take it,
For you shall not plead in vain.'

XVII

So, with eager hand approaching,
He stooped low to pick the rose,
When a serpent, coiled beneath it,
Did his fiery eyes disclose.

XVIII

Then I, shivering, started forward,
All my heart with anguish torn :
' Leave the roses for the lilies ;
They have neither sting nor thorn.'

XIX

But he drew me close beside him,
And he whispered in my ear
Words that I, another's warden,
Might not, ought not, dared not, hear.

XX

How I wrung my hands in sorrow,
    How my heart ached with despair,
How I prayed to God to help me,
    How He heard my frantic prayer,

XXI

Is a tale that ne'er was spoken ;
    But the pilgrim since that day
Has not sought my master's roses,
    Has not even passed this way.

XXII

Now to other wardens say I—
    For I've won the right to speak
By the anguish of my spirit
    And the pallor of my cheek—

XXIII

King or prince, or who he may be
    That to thee doth trust confide,
Leave no pilgrim in the precincts,
    At his will to wander wide.

XXIV

Pick no pansies, no, nor lilies,
    To adorn another's breast
Than the one who is thy master,
    If thy conscience would have rest ;

XXV

For no pilgrim but will wander
    Where the owner's roses bloom,
When the lilies and the pansies
    Lose for him their faint perfume.

C

THE WEB OF LIFE.

My life, which was so straight and plain,
Has now become a tangled skein,
　Yet God still holds the thread ;
Weave as I may, His hand doth guide
The shuttle's course, however wide
　The chain in woof be wed.

One weary night, when years went by,
I plied my loom with tear and sigh,
　In grief unnamed, untold ;
But when at last the morning's light
Broke on my vision, pure and bright
　There gleamed a cloth of gold.

And now I never lose my trust,
Weave as I may—and weave I must—
　That God doth hold the thread ;
He guides my shuttle on its way,
He makes complete my task each day ;
　What more, then, can be said ?

THE MAIDEN'S FLOWER OMENS.

I

' If he bring me a rose, a briar rose,
  To place in my braided hair,
I shall know there are thorns in life for me
  And many a wearying care.

' If he bring me a lily pure and pale
  And lay it upon my breast,
I shall know that my life will be of peace,
  As a bird in its mother's nest.

' If he bring me pansies purple and gold
  And clasp them within my hand,
I shall know that rare treasures I will glean
  From many a distant land.

' If he bring me orange blossoms sweet,
  With their clinging buds beside,
I shall know that before the year is out
  I will surely be his bride.

'If he bring me blue forget-me-nots,
  As blue as the summer sky,
I shall know I will never falsehood see
  In the blue of his bonnie eye.

'If he bring me poppies red as the coals
  That glow in the blacksmith's fire,
I shall know like the coals his love will die
  In the ashes of his desire.

'If he bring me soft carnation pinks
  In a wreath as children wear,
I shall know it is but fancy for me,
  That with others I must share.

'If he bring me snowdrops waxen white
  That droop with their own weight low,
I will know, alas! when the winter comes
  I shall sleep beneath the snow.'

II

Nor snowdrops white, nor pinks, nor blossoms pale,
  Were given to the maiden fair ;
Nor poppies red, nor blue forget-me-nots,
  Nor pansies yet, nor lilies rare ;

But laden down with roses came he then—
Moss-roses, maiden-blush and white,
Burgundy roses crimson as the wine
When crystal goblets flash the light;

Roses, like sea shells, with pink pearly tints,
Roses with petals of rare yellow gold,
Roses as scarlet as a woman's lips
When rain warm kisses all untold.

He flung them o'er her, laughing as they fell.
No laughter rippled back to him :
'I hold an omen in these flowers,' she said,
'An omen for the future dim.

'Would you had brought me lilies in their stead,
Or pansies with their hearts of gold,
Or dear forget-me-nots, that breathe of faith,
Seeming some sacred trust to hold!

'But roses! roses with their cruel thorns!
Oft-times as false as fair are they,
Since canker-worms coil close within their hearts,
Eating their fragrant life away.'

III

'Sad is the life where roses do not bloom ;
  And one forgives the thorns,' he said,
'When one has drunken of the rich perfume
  That regal roses always shed.

'I bring thee roses as unto a queen.
  If thou, sweet love, my queen wilt be,
Only the roses shalt thou have in life,
  And all the thorns shall be for me.'

She heard, and straight upon his breast she hid
  Her happy face, with blushes warm.
Her trusting heart believed the words he said ;
  He felt her answer in her clinging form.

No fairer bride e'er orange blossoms wore
  Than this sweet maid at chancel rail ;
No husband fond so kept the vows he made—
  Yet thorns with roses, reader, never fail.

BLOSSOMS AND THORNS.

UP to the courts of heaven fair
  A spirit sped one day ;
Released from earth, the spirit cried,
  ' Open the gate, I pray ! '

An angel swung the golden door ;
  ' Where is thy cross ? ' he said.
' Here is my crown ; I have no cross
  To offer in its stead.'

' No cross, no crown,' the answer made,
  And slowly turned the door ;
The pilgrim spirit bowed her head
  As one in sorrow sore.

' Dear Lord ! ' she cried, in her despair,
  ' Shut not the gate on me ;
Thorns are within the crown I wear
  Like those that piercèd Thee.'

Then quickly swung the gate again ;
　　Our Lord Himself was there,
Whose ears are never, never closed
　　Unto a sufferer's prayer.

' Woman, give Me your crown,' He said ;
　　' If martyr's thorns you wear,
You can pass in the golden gate
　　With those who crosses bear.'

Then from her drooping head she took
　　Its crown of blossoms bright ;
And, lo ! the piercing points within
　　Revealed themselves to sight.

' Why hast thou worn this crown ?' He asked ;
　　' Better a cross to bear.'
' I wore it, Lord, for love of him
　　Who made and placed it there.'

' For love like this,' our Saviour said,
　　' Though to the creature given,
Thou hast done well to call on Me,
　　For thou hast won thy heaven.'

THE MAGDALENE.

SUGGESTED BY A PAINTING OF A MAGDALENE.

Luke vii. 47.

BENEATH a sacred shrine she kneeled,
Her bosom's charms scarce half concealed,
'Tween flowing robe and hair revealed—

Hair of the hue of burnished gold,
Rippling along the dark blue fold
That wrapped a form of peerless mould.

' Oh, Christ!' she cried, 'here at Thy feet
I leave my tears, for tears are meet
For one who findeth sin so sweet!

' And yet, dear Lord, I love not sin,
And Thou, who readest hearts within,
See'st my soul doth oftenest win!

' But when his lips my own lips press
In royal bliss of tenderness,
Such as the angels cannot guess,

'Then sin no longer sin doth seem,
And wrapped as in a holy dream
I give my very self to him :

'I give, and weep I have no more
To give to him whom I adore,
And count my life of little store.

'If life for him I could but yield,
Nor priest to shrive, but unannealed,
I'd walk alone the shadowy field.

'To give him heaven I would dwell
Where, in rank groves of asphodel,
Tread spirits that from heaven fell.

'Forgive me, Lord, in that I love,
Nor close Thy courts to me above
If sinless in all else I prove !'

Low fell her head upon her breast
When thus her sin she had confest,
Nor seen one pausing there to rest—

A pilgrim father in his gown,
Dusty and travel-stained and worn ;
And as he heard the tears ran down,

' Daughter,' he said, ' thou art the snare
That Satan sets for a soul rare
Which nought could tempt that is less fair.

' If thou wouldst save it for Christ's fold,
Cut close thy hair of yellow gold
And change thy raiment new for old.

' Still more : thy love thou must conceal,
Indifference must feign to feel.
The task is hard, but for his weal

' Thy love thou canst forego, and bear
Pangs which at first he too will share,
But in the end the crown will wear

' Which saints and martyrs only gain
When torture fires and racks of pain
Have cleansed their souls from every stain.

' This crown can come through thee alone.
Bear thou thy cross and make no moan ;
So shalt thou all thy sins atone.'

She cut her hair of gleaming gold,
She clothed herself in sackcloth old,
She said, ' My pulses have grown cold ;

' I love but God alone.'   He heard,
Her lover fond, whose blood was stirred
Like quivering flame at every word.

' What lying priest hath wrought me this,
To rob me of the heavenly bliss
For which I gladly heaven would miss ?

' Not for thy locks of virgin gold,
Not for thy garment's purple fold,
Do I thy supple beauty hold

' Above all joys of earth or heaven ;
And though my sins were seven times seven
Thy love would prove the saving leaven ! '

Her eyes told what no words confest,
' If love will save thee thou art blest ;'
Firm as a saint she said the rest :

' Go ! follow duty day by day !
Since thou art saved if I obey
I will not lead thy soul astray.

' Then at our death we shall be shriven ;
Through Hades we shall pass to heaven ;
Since unto such as love too much
Much also is forgiven.'

CHAFF AND WHEAT.

'The blows that strike deepest into the heart are struck by
human hands which we have loved and trusted.'

My heart lay on the threshing-floor :
　　I stifled every wail
As blow on blow descended
　　From one who held the flail.

My heart lay on the threshing-floor,
　　But it was not in vain ;
The chaff was scattered to the winds
　　In hours of keenest pain.

My heart lay on the threshing-floor ;
　　Yet, bruisèd though it be,
It still a worthy offering is
　　To thee, beloved, to thee !

Then take it now and guard it well,
　　Dear love, for love of me :
My heart lay on the threshing-floor
　　That it might worthier be.

LOVE AND FAME.

'To be great is to be exposed to all the shafts of envy ; but to love is to wear an " armour against fate." '

I DREAMED.

Before me stood a vision bright,
A creature of celestial light,
Of glorious mien and mould.
Her velvet robe, with hem of gold,
Fell to her feet in graceful fold,
Gleaming with jewels rare and cold.
Her dark hair shaded lovely eyes,
Which flashed like stars in midnight skies,
While, stately as a crownèd queen,
She wore her wreath of laurel green.
In reverence I bowed my head,
And saw, low kneeling by my bed,
A gentler, fairer, sylph-like form,
Whose eyes with love were beaming warm.
She spoke—her voice was sweetly low ;
In silver tones it seemed to flow :

' Turn not away from heart like mine:
   With pulses warm and true ;
Turn not away that glance of thine
   Though bright yon form to view.
Her path is through a weary way ;
   Sharp thorns will pierce thy feet,
And falsely flatt'ring is the lay
   Thy list'ning ear will greet.
The canker eateth at her heart,
   It gnaweth to the core ;
Oh, bid her from thy side depart   .
   And never tempt thee more.
There's poison in the laurel leaf
   That's braided in her hair ;
Her very smile will bring thee grief,
   Although it seems so fair.
Thy brightest hopes will all decay,
   Thy joys to ashes turn,
While in thy breast with fitful sway
   Their smouldering embers burn.'
The low voice ceased.   I raised my eyes
From hers, as blue as azure skies,
And turned them from her glance so warm
Upon the stately, radiant form.

The dark eyes smiled—entrancing gaze !
How fast my heart beat 'neath their rays !
The red lips moved—melodious flow !
Deep-toned as bugle notes drawn low,
They thrilled my heart with bounding
  throe.
    ' My name is Fame,' the goddess said ;
      ' My mission unto thee.
    A glory round thy path I'll shed
      If thou wilt go with me.
    The way is steep, a stony path ;
      But, when we gain the end,
    I'll crown with glittering coronal
      The brow that thou wilt bend.
    The world will turn an envious gaze
      Upon thy lofty height,
    And thou shalt proudly meet those rays
      And glory in thy might.
    Then come with me ; leave yonder fay
      To minds of meaner mould ;
    Come, on our path away, away,
      Success awaits the bold.'
That clarion voice awoke a lyre ;
It filled my veins with molten fire

As one by one its chords were swept.
I turned to Love ; she, kneeling, wept ;
Her lashes long drooped low with tears,
And 'neath their lids were boding fears.
' Look ere we part,' she sighing said ;
And then her hand my vision led ;
I saw through fields of pulsing air
A pathway radiantly fair :
Green were the grots and mossy glades,
Cool flowed the rills in greener shades,
And wild flowers grew in tangled maze
Beneath the thick vine's arching ways.
The velvet turf was gemmed with dew,
And starry flowers of every hue,
And flute-like voices stirred the air
From loving lips of beings fair.
The path swept to a river's side,
Where timidly upon the tide,
With foot advanced, its power they tried ;
The amber wavelets gently bore
The spirit forms from verdant shore :
And oh ! entrancing, rapturous sight !
The banks beyond of crystal bright,

Wreathed with rich vines of emerald green,
And flowers so rare no eye hath seen,
And gates of sapphire and of gold,
And streets of pearl, and fountains cold,
While angel forms came forth to greet
The angel spirits which they meet.
' I'll go with thee, dear Love,' I cried ;
And still for glorious Fame I sighed.
Love marked the wildly-heaving sighs,
She saw the tears gleam in my eyes,
And, pointing with her faultless hand,
Said, ' Look at yonder toiling band.'
I looked ; and lo ! 'midst rocks and briers,
'Midst nameless graves and funeral pyres,
Fame's toil-worn band were struggling on
Beneath the fierce rays of the sun—
No mossy glades, no vine-arched ways,
To shelter them from burning rays ;
Their sunken eyes gleamed wild and strange,
And frequent looks of hate exchanged.
Upward and onward still they pressed,
While some, more weary than the rest,
Found by the way an unknown grave,
For not one stopped to soothe or save,

But, often trampling on the weak,
The highest place they seemed to seek.
They paused not for the dying wail,
The cheek so wan, so ashen pale ;
And, shuddering at the fearful sight,
I turned away in dread affright.
For Fame no more my spirit sighed ;
Ambition's power that moment died.
I follow Love, and Fame may flee—
No longer she hath charms for me.
Pale Envy's shafts at her are borne,
While Love escapes with armour worn
That clothes the form from crown to heel,
Invulnerable as proven steel.

THE SOUL'S CITADEL.

FROM AN UNPUBLISHED NOVEL.

I STOOD upon the heights of Love :
  The air was passion-free ;
I thought not of the things of Time,
  But of Eternity.

And he who led me to those heights,
  And bade me scale its walls,
I looked upon as on a god,
  As free from earthly thralls.

I scaled the walls, I reached the tower,
  I flung my flag on high ;
I thought I heard the angels call
  As breeze on breeze swept by.

My head was strong, my heart was brave,
  My vision keen and clear ;
I saw the ways the saints have trod,
  I felt their spirits near.

What foe would dare in hours like these
   A soul so clad assail?
Ah, woe is me! no foe but he
   Who helped me don my mail.

His hand struck low in cruel blow
   The one whose feet he'd led
From level plains to mountain-tops,
   And left me as one dead.

But still I hold my pure white flag,
   Though low in dust I lie;
I hear the breezes out of heaven
   Still murmur, murmur by.

And now 'tis given me to know,
   And see with spirit's eyes,
That Christ alone can lead our souls
   Up into Paradise.

THE STORY OF MY LOVE.

WHEN the lilacs were in bloom,
    And the skies were soft and pale,
I told my love the story
    As we walked in Thornleydale ;
Oh, the aisles of lilac bloom
    In the green and lovely vale
Where I walked with Maud at morn,
    And she listened to my tale.

Twice six moons had waxed and waned,
    Twice six months had passed away,
Ere I begged my Maud to name
    Very near our wedding day.
So we walked in Thornleydale,
    While she, blushing, hung her head :
The moss roses on the bush
    Blush not half so sweet a red.

When the locusts were in bloom,
   Lilies pure and snowdrops pale,
With my bride upon my arm
   I went out from Thornleydale;
Tender eyes were raised to mine,
   Tender lips to mine were pressed,
And I bore my bride away
   From her fair and flowery nest.

When the winter skies were grey,
   And the snow lay in the vale,
When the winds were bleak and wild,
   We came back to Thornleydale;
But the tender eyes were closed,
   And the tender lips were cold;
And my baby and my bride
   Sleep together side by side.

THE CUP OF LIFE.

I HOLD with trembling hand the full, rich cup
Which God has given unto me to drink—
Such generous dole that not one added drop
Could fall within and not o'erbrim its wealth.
I would my hold were stronger, but, alas!
The strongest arm is weak indeed against
The purposes of God.   Ah! blest be he
Who still can give God thanks when all the wine
Life yields is spilled, and nought is left but lees.
Couldst thou, my heart?   What didst thou do but
    moan
When on a time a north-east wind did breathe
Upon thy calm, vexing thy life with plaints
That would have best befit a tempest storm?
But now the wind has lulled, 'tis well and wise
To search thy soul and question of its strength,
That if again a few drops from thy cup
Are swept unto the ground, thou shalt not grieve

As if the richness of thy draught were gone.
Take time to thank thy God for what He leaves,
Faint heart, and thou wilt find the hours grow few
Wherein thou mournest over what He takes.

REAL AND IDEAL.

No storied castle's window owns a view
　　Fairer than mine that overlooks the west ;
Rolling between are countless waves of blue,
　　Bearing white sails unto their ports of rest.

Here slopes the orchard with its wealth of bloom,
　　The cattle grazing to the water's edge ;
There stroll fair children on the shell-strewn beach,
　　Or watch the scene from yon bold, beetling ledge.

Now curves the sinuous rock-bound coast away,
　　Or reaches out in promontories fair,
While far beyond the tireless billows play
　　And toss their white arms in the golden air.

Nearer, a meadow rolls its emerald sward,
　　Flecked with white clover as with pearls of Ind,
Its huge breast scarred with timbers of the nord—
　　Wrecks driven on shore in gales of adverse wind.

Where walls of rock relentless keep at bay
   The reckless waves that chafe against their sides,
Fall glowing showers of soft prismatic spray :
   As ceaseless break the never-resting tides.

I close my eyes : the meadow, coast, and wave,
   Like phantom pictures fade and disappear ;
Sweet absent faces gather round my own,
   And clinging hands clasp mine which are not
      here.

NEWPORT.

WORDS.

WHEN thought holds empire in the brain of man,
And deeds unworthy we are brought to scan,
How leaps the soul with indignation stung!
How words that burn find utterance on the tongue!
When Treachery strikes the heart with coward
    blow,
And Falsehood strives her subtle dart to throw,
The soul speaks up most nobly in its scorn,
Unless its clay be but ignobly born.
Not so when love falls wounded to the dust,
Smitten by hands it only knew to trust;
Words then are worthless to the anguished mind;
Save 'Help us, God,' no other words we find;
And but His strength upheld us in our need
We would be weak and powerless indeed.

DRIFTED AWAY.

In the morn of life I anchored a barque
  By some isles I was sure would stay ;
Alas ! alas ! in the treacherous dark
  My green isles drifted away.

And now I look back on their groves of palm,
  Their fountains of solace and joy,
As martyrs look for the life beyond
  When flames and the rack destroy.

Bore ever a martyr a keener pain
  Than our Lord when deserted knew ?
Can the fire scorch as burns the thought,
  ' I trusted to love not true ' ?

Come back, come back, my beautiful isles,
  That I anchored my barque beside ;
No other isles like my isles of palms
  In the tropic seas so wide !

Ah, when once an isle has drifted away,
  Nor fountains nor palms remain.
My anchor swings loose to lodge as it may ;
  My barque is at sea again.

RESIGNATION.

SHE heard the anguished wail of those whose hearts
Are broken on God's wheels, and when she said
To him who led her steps, 'Why bring me here?'
He answered, 'Have no fear; I do but lead
Where He directs who knows the path you need.'
Her trembling heart in terror tried to turn;
But flaming swords, the ministers of fate,
For ever held her back, nor ceased pursuit
Until upon the rack, her heart, bound fast,
Writhing in torture lay.   Her ashen lips
Refused to say, 'Thy will, my God, be done!'
And only murmured, 'Thine, O God, the power!'
Then groaned the wheel, revolving round,
Till drop by drop the blood no longer flowed;
For first like gushing fountains it poured forth,
Showering accusing spray in drops on those
Who lent their strength to turn its ponderous weight.
With life at lowest ebb God's angels came,
And one, whose face was radiant with peace,

Lifted her up and said, ' Come now with us,
Nor grudge the pain that wrung unwilling drops
From thy heart's core, since unto thee is given
To walk on earth with angels sent from heaven.'

THE ARMOUR OF LOVE.

'I pity, I forgive, I forget.'—LOUIS XVIII.

YOU ask me whence the armour came
That steeled me through those days to live
He sent it who has taught me since
  To pity and forgive.

You ask me how I bore the cross
Ere recompensing crown was set ;
I like not to recall those hours :
  Would that I could forget !

You tell me now I know my friends ;
I knew them all, dear love, before ;
The phalanx never broke nor swayed
  That Friendship's banner bore

You tell me that henceforth my life
Is freed from Envy's vengeful eye.
Believe it not ; till heaven is gained
  Her arrows still will fly.

E

But yet one word for you I have :
This armour that's around me wrought
Not only keeps her shafts from me,
    But makes them all as nought.

Draw as she may her monstrous bow,
With poisoned arrows basely set,
They cannot pierce the mail I wear,
    Since now I pity and forget.

PEACE THAT PASSETH UNDER-
STANDING.

WHAT land of promise this that now I tread
What skies are these that, arching o'er my head,
Seem full of angel faces looking down,
As close I hold Love's sceptre and Love's crown ?
I have not crossed the barrier stream of death ;
Still does the mortal hold within its sheath
Its spirit body as the ripened husk its wheat ;
Still this sweet world I walk with clinging feet,
Loth to depart, yet longing still to go ;
Two natures warring each with each still flow
Like tides that now advance and now recede,
As earth attracts or heaven's voices lead.
The answer comes as if from God's white throne :
' Here dwell those hearts which my great peace
        have known.'

THE STRANGER.

'Abide with us; for it is toward evening, and the day is far spent.'—LUKE xxiv. 29.

THE morning splendours of my life have flown,
  The noontide glories now are on the wane ;
I walk the path to Emmaus all alone,
  And think o'er 'things that happened' once again.

Who is the stranger joins me on the way,
  Teaching me truths which make my heart to glow ?
O Lord, reveal Thy face to me, I pray ;
  If Thou art with me, give me sight to know

So the apostles walked with Him of old,
  And knew Him not until they sat at meat.
Methinks my loving heart would soon have told,
  Had I been there when He drew near to greet

I will not let a doubt within my soul
  That it is other than the Lord I love.
He leads me onward to yon distant goal ;
  I see the lights far streaming from above.

Abide with me ! my day is wellnigh spent ;
  The night of death, dear Lord, will soon be
      here ;
If on Thy breast whene'er the message's sent,
  What will I know of darkness or of fear ?

The morning splendours of my life have flown
  Its noontide glories now are on the wane ;
I walk the path to Emmaus *not* alone,
  For He is with me who of old was slain.

A PICTURE.

ONLY a churchyard covered with snow,
    A church in a lonely dale ;
There gleamed in the west a golden glow,
    The heavens above were pale.

The sentinel trees, like shades of the dead,
    Stood up stark against the sky :
Their frozen branches at rest were spread,
    For no winds went surging by.

The ground was white as the pure cold face
    That sleeps in its coffin-bed ;
A holy stillness was in the place
    That comes only to the dead.

To a longing wild my soul gave birth
    In that solemn peace to share,
To be done with the harsh turmoils of earth,
    Their pain and their wearying care.

'Would I were at rest!' As the words arose,
  They died on my lips unsaid :
It seemed a sin before God to breathe
  I envied the buried dead.

I thought of him who stood by my side,
  The trials he had to bear,
Of the tender trust he had placed in me,
  Of the grief I had to share.

I wished no more for the frozen sleep
  Of the churchyard white and lone,
Where the ghostly trees their vigils keep,
  And winds in the midnight moan.

The picture hangs now in memory's hall—
  The churchyard covered with snow ;
And it holds my soul within its thrall
  In a spell that none can know.

'WOULD I WERE AT REST.'

'He chooseth best
Who chooseth labour instead of rest.'
H. B. BOSTWICK.

NO readiness to die so pleaseth God
  As readiness to live to do God's will:
He measureth unto us appointed days;
  Our round of duties we have yet to fill.

Shrink not the task!   We can the victory win.
  Our fetters strong?   Our souls are stronger yet.
God did but fashion this pulsating clay
  In which the jewel of the soul to set.

That has dominion over flesh and sin.
  If the sore struggle be but once begun,
He'll give His angels charge concerning us
  Until the final victory be won.

Then let our lives a daily offering be;

The incense sweet unto our God shall rise;

The contrite spirit and the humble heart

He loveth better than the sacrifice.

LEAVING STOCKHOLM, MARCH 1874.

O WINGÈD winds! bear on the hours
 Which now for days must roll,
Dragging their weary length along
 Like nights within the pole—

The Arctic pole, where never sun
 Illumes for months the sea,
Though brightly shine the stars above,
 The stars of destiny.

In them I'll trust, for God is just,
 And orders all aright;
He holds the stars within their course
 From darkness unto light.

The winter goes, the summer comes,
 Then steadfast shines the sun;
For all the wintry nights are o'er
 And wintry days are done.

Now unto my desponding soul
Its dearest hope I'll hold—
That steadfast love may centre round
The darlings of my fold ;

That they may know no wintry days,
No nights of dark despair ;
But o'er the tropic seas of love
Float into havens fair.

When winter goes, may summer come,
And steadfast shine the sun,
And all the wintry days be o'er,
And wintry nights be done.

MIDWAY.

MIDWAY upon Life's sea my bark speeds on ;
Steeped with the noontide's gold, the cradled crests
I turn to look upon lie still as babes
Upon their mother's breast. Ah! once it was
Not thus.   I know a time when wild storms raged,
And thick clouds swept athwart the sky, until
The waves, high tossed, in murky blackness fumed.
Some treasure from my hold I lost ere those
Rough waves grew calm ; some garnered hopes,
    some faith,
Some trust, went down, and for my loss my soul
Sent up a cry which might have pierced the
    heavens,
So sharp its agony.   But now the sea
Holds not one trace of all that wild turmoil.
I stand and gaze upon its vast expanse,
And strive to keep in view the far-off shore,
Which to my sight grows dimmer every hour—
The shore whereon I lingered ere my sails

Were trimmed, for pastime gathering pebble stones,
Which, Midas-touched, have turned since then to
 gold.
What of the land beyond ? A dim grey haze
Rolls dense between, which, when the storms
 come on,
Lifts for a space, swift driven before the wind,
Revealing glimpses of a glorious haven.

* * * * * * * *

I fear not tempests nor the blasts of cold
That sweep from frozen zones; these have no power;
But when I slowly drift through odorous groves
Of spice, soft languors wooing me to stay,
'Tis then I fear ; for if I leave my helm
For dalliance in those bowers, against some rock
It straight may graze, and leave a shattered bark,
Which, if I trust, will founder on the deep ;
Or if, at most, it bear me into port,
How would I dread to render my account
To Him who trusted to my hands the bark
He fashioned with such care, for purpose wise
And kind! O Father! grant through storm and calm
I still may near those shores where evermore
Thy angels stand to lead us up to Thee.

TO ONE WHO DISLIKES FLOWERS.

WHAT memories bring they unto thee,
   That thou shouldst turn from flowers ?
What memories from beyond the sea,
   From thy far northern bowers ?
Ah! well I know some mighty grief
   Hath crushed from out thy soul
The love thou surely must have felt
   Ere girlhood won its goal.
Say not that they were never dear :
   I could not bear that sound ;
'Twould break the atmosphere of light
   That now enfolds thee round.

I'd rather think some sacred grief,
   Some buried love, may be,
Which, linked in memory with flowers,
   Springs up in agony
Whene'er their gentle breath sweeps near,
   Or when thy true eyes rest

Upon Earth's sweet and stainless buds,
   Her holiest gift, her best.
The 'jasmine' sweet, blue violets wild,
   I plucked with tender care,
Mingling their bloom with brighter hues,
   Exotics wondrous, rare.
I thought to see thee bend those eyes,
   So glorious in their light,
Most fondly o'er the treasured flowers ;
   But to my questioning sight
There came no pleasure to thy lips,
   No smile within thy eyes,
And coldly, coldly to my heart
   I held its great surprise.
The world may whisper thoughts unkind,
   But ne'er will I believe
Other than this : that thy strong heart
   In bitterness doth grieve
O'er some sad memory of the past,
   Some faded human flower,
For which of love thou still hast kept
   A more than regal dower.

DESERTED.

ALL night upon my bed I toss,
  All day I sigh and moan ;
Ah ! wherefore should I break my heart
  Against a heart of stone ?

She rolleth past me in the street
  With all her pomp and show,
She leaneth on her cushioned seat
  Unmindful of my woe.

Oh, cursed be he who came between
  With his ill-gotten gold !
Oh, cursed—But no ; I dare not curse
  The mother who hath sold

Her daughter's form without her heart.
  My God ! that form so fair
Which I had thought to call my own,
  And all my pleasures share !

But neither gold nor gems were mine ;
   Yet with her by my side
I would have won a prince's dower
   To deck my bonnie bride.

Alas ! alas! what need have I
   To struggle with these hands ?
Without her smiles, oh what to me
   Are untold gold or lands ?

Oh, cursed—No, no; I will not curse :
   Peace rest with thee, my love;
Let me the only sufferer be,
   Poor caged and pinioned dove.

Though other arms your form enfold,
   I know within your breast
The memory of our hallowed days
   Must there for ever rest.

And though you school your eyes to scorn,
   And check the heaving sigh,
There cannot be but tears for me
   When others are not nigh.

F

A VALENTINE.

FAIR as the vestals, as serenely cold
　　Art thou, sweet maiden, with thy eyes of blue ;
Thy tresses long, in waves of burnished gold,
　　Cast shadows o'er a cheek of rose-leaf hue.

The silken lashes of thy violet eyes
　　Drop with a sunny curve from snowy lid,
Half shading all the purity that lies
　　Within their quiet depths so sweetly hid.

The matchless arching of thy ruby lip,
　　The glittering pearls thy smile discloses,
Thy mouth fresh as the dew the flowers sip,
　　And redolent of sweets as budding roses—

Too fair for my unskilful hand to trace,
　　Never a poet could thy charms combine,
Nor artist draw thee in thy winning grace
　　Unless a monarch of his art divine.

For such a boon how dare my heart aspire?
   Trembling, I bring its wealth of love to thee ;
No Persian worshipper of flaming fire
   E'er bent his god a more devoted knee.

IN EGYPT.

MY childhood's dream, the Orient reached,
  Why yearns my heart for home?
And why across the throbbing seas
  Do all my fancies roam?

Never before, except in dreams
  Or painter's glowing skill,
Such scenes have broken on my eyes
  Or made my pulses thrill.

Oh, witching hours! oh, days of light!
  Oh, nights of solemn calm
That float us down the storied Nile,
  Along its groves of palm!

Here Moses lived, and Joseph ruled,
  And Israel pitched his tent;
Here came the Virgin with her Child,
  By angel voices sent.

Here art and science made their home,
  And skill and power reared
The monuments that mock at time,
  In grandeur vast and weird.

But though their majesty I feel,
  Still yearns my heart for home,
And still across the throbbing seas
  Will all my fancies roam.

THEBES, *February* 1866.

TO A STUDENT.

I HAD a dream for thee when thou wert young,
For e'er thy boyhood's years were scarcely told
I marked thy worth, and felt my pulses thrill
With thoughts of what thy future might reveal.
Press on, and make that vision of my mind
Complete.   Press on, and scale those battlements
Wherefrom the conqueror looks forth on fields
Unstained with blood, elate with victory
Such as crowned emperors who spent their days
In carnage never knew.   Elate, and yet
As humble as a child.   No fruitless tears,
Like those that Alexander shed of old,
For other worlds to win ; for whoso takes
That wondrous citadel can from its walls
Count tier on tier of battlements to scale
Before his eager eyes will scan the broad
Arcana of great Nature's laws.   And thus
The conqueror grows a child, and wears with grac
The garments of humility.   'Tis those,

And only those, who in dark trenches make

Faint passes with a play-time sword, nor reach

Beyond, who boast their prowess.   Take thou
heed :

Sleep not upon thy post, so thou wouldst prove

Thyself a warrior worthy of the cause.

God give thee armour proof against assault

In whatsoever guise it come to thee,

Rounding thy life with every joy that makes

Complete the days of man, and grant that when

Thou layest down thy helmet and thy steel

'Twill be to take up worthier beyond.

MY HEART.

My heart is like a wild bird;
  'Tis ever on the wing,
Soaring amidst the amber clouds,
  A wild and wayward thing,
Or stooping to the green earth
  To nestle in some flower,
Or singing sadly all the day
  In some neglected bower.

My heart is like the wild wind;
  It flitteth here and there—
Now wailing o'er some ruined shrine,
  Some cloister dim and bare,
Or laughing with the sunny sky,
  Or dancing with the rills,
Or sweeping through the brave old woods
  That crown the mossy hills.

My heart is like the wild stream
  That glideth through the vale,

Where grow the meek-eyed violets,
  The lilies pure and pale ;
Oh, this is what my heart is like,
  For, ever mirrored there,
Is some dear, stainless, cherished flower,
  Some bright bud sweet and fair.

And 'tis not like the wild bird,
  And 'tis not like the wind ;
The bird is faithless to the flowers,
  Nor trust nor love can bind.
The wind full oft doth break their hearts,
  Surely they fade though slow ;
But the glad stream is always true
  To the flowers drooping low.

ANTICIPATION.

OH, hasten on, ye loitering hours!
  I long once more to see
The valley of my childhood's home,
  The mountains and the lea ;
The feathery groves that crown the hills,
  Or droop beside the stream ;
The meadows green, the murmuring rills,
  Where dewy violets gleam ;
The winding path around the lake
  Where water lilies float,
And spread at eve their stainless sails
  Like some sweet fairy boat ;
The dark grey rocks that on me frowned
  From mountain ramparts bold,
The placid stream that glides below
  Over its sands of gold ;
The village church with towering spire,
  The elms upon 'the green ; '
The homesteads with their garden walks,
  And verdant lawns between.

All, all, my fancy longs to see,
  Each spot within that vale ;
The graveyard with its mossy stones,
  And sculptured marbles pale.
All hold for me their memories
  Sacred as saintly shrines,
And like a pilgrim's longing heart
  My heart with longing pines.
But like a pilgrim at a tomb
  In silence I should bow,
If midst those scenes and in those haunts
  My feet should wander now.
Yet hasten on, ye loitering hours,
  That I may once more see
The valley of my childhood's home
  Ere earth is nought to me.
And when my busy brain is still,
  My heart has ceased to beat,
Then take me back, and bury me
  Where roamed my childish feet ;
And write upon a simple stone,
  That those who pass may read :
' *She was well loved* by God and man
  In hour of sorest need.'

BETRAYED.

SLOWLY stern Winter treads our hill-girt vale,
  His regal brow with hoary locks encrowned ;
Through leafless trees he breathes a dirge-like
      wail,
  And the far hills repeat the mournful sound.

The bright-eyed flowers have paled beside the
    stream
  That winds across the fields its fitful way,
But from the woods I catch a crimson gleam
  Deep as the glowing hues of dying day.

'Tis where the pliant vine entwines the oak,
  Then upward climbs, wreathing from bough to
      bough,
Falling beside the roof whose curling smoke
  Alone I see above the forest now.

Thick gleam the sprays with coral berries fair,
    Its leaves as glossy as June laurels be ;
I knew a maid who ofttimes in her hair
    Braided its clusters all too carefully.

It is a story long and full of grief,
    That on this page I would not care to tell.
She faded with the summer flowers brief,
    When autumn's frosts first on their beauty fell.

Ah ! where is he who cast this deadly blight ?
    Hath he no share in sorrow he hath wrought ?
Can he escape the voice within by flight—
    The memories with such desolation fraught ?

Breathe to him, winter winds, of all the woe
    The mother feels within her lonely cot ;
Leave the new grave beside the river's flow,
    And whisper of the clay he hath forgot.

Oh, haunt him with thy wail, thou winter wind,
    And fill his sinful heart with boding fear ;
Give him no rest, let him no mercy find,
    Until he sheds the penitential tear.

Perchance it may some other victim save
 That even now his passion marks for prey ;
For little cares he, so that in the grave
 His sins are hidden from the light of day.

O Earth ! so fair art thou we scarce can dream
 Of all the sorrows hid within thy breast,
The broken hearts that cross dark Lethe's stream
 Ere thy fond bosom folds them to their rest.

Rest to the dust consigned unto thy care,
 While, far from thee, the spirit wings its way,
Fettered no more by chains it erst did wear
 Within its helpless tenement of clay.

Wail on, ye winter winds, above the dead ;
 Ye cannot wake her from her dreamless sleep ;
Soft is the pillow to her wearied head,
 For ever closed the eyes that once did weep.

A GIFT OF FLOWERS.

O FLOWERS of wondrous loveliness !
   What mem'ries strange arise
As all your beauty rich and rare
   I drink with eager eyes !

O meadows of my childhood's home !
   O forests dark and deep !
O mountains where I used to roam
   Far up the rock-crowned steep !

I see them all ; I feel the wind
   Playing amid my hair ;
I even scent the very breath
   Of violets on the air.

No others have seemed half so sweet
   Since from that spot I strayed ;
No others half so fair to me
   As those in that wild glade.

I hear the babbling torrent leap,
  I feel a hand in mine ;
Again I stray in those green paths
  As once in 'auld lang syne.'

But heavy, heavy grows the air,
  A mist creeps o'er my view ;
Dear saints ! I see my buried friend :
  Those are her eyes of blue !

Ah me ! ah me ! 'twas but a dream :
  The flowers alone remain ;
She knoweth all the bliss of heaven,
  And·I of earth the pain.

The pain !   What said I, when my friends
  Strew o'er my path with flowers ?
Ah !   earth hath very much of joy
  To bless our passing hours.

And though these flowers fair will droop
  And wither soon away,
I shall keep always in my heart
  The fragrance of this day.

THE FAITHLESS LOVER.

'There, there will be neither marrying nor giving in marriage,
for we shall all be like the angels of God.'

SWEETEST Marion, wilt thou listen
　While my soul calls out for thine?
Canst thou listen from high heaven
　To this longing prayer of mine?
Oh, my love, am I no longer
　Friend of friends, dear one, to thee?
Can I have no word of answer?
　Speak, pure soul, oh speak to me!

By our long and fond communings,
　By remorseful pangs I feel,
By the gnawings of this serpent
　In the wounds that will not heal,
By my love so strong and deathless,
　Though so faithless in that hour
When Ambition's torch did lure me,
　Held by hands that knew its power,

G

Bend thine earnest eyes upon me—
   Eyes so pure I can but weep
When I think that earth hath lost them,
   Well-like eyes so clear and deep.
Earth hath lost them, heaven hath gained them ;
   Oh, come back, thou angel form,
And my soul will go to meet thee
   From this world of grief and storm.

Ah! I cannot feel thy presence :
   Death keeps guard between us now ;
He hath clasped thee since we parted,
   He hath kissed thy placid brow.
Death and falsehood came between us,
   But my spirit still is thine ;
And I know I am forgiven,
   Though I have no word nor sign.

When long years have passed before me,
   And my penance days are done,
I will seek through worlds eternal
   Till I find thee, cherished one.
There we'll need no vain betrothal,
   Like God's angels we shall be ;
In thy eyes I'll read my pardon,
   Thou in mine my love for thee.

THE ENTHUSIAST.

O CRUEL heart that would my heart lay bare,
And seek with earthly love to spread a snare!
O spirit strong that would my spirit thrall,
And chain to earth its hopes and longings all!

I know thy power, yet hold myself to be
Able to triumph o'er the world and thee,
Renouncing earthly love if need require,
For in my heart there glows a holier fire.

Though troublous sorrows compass me around,
Though grief should leave its ever-bleeding wound,
Yet still my chosen path I'll persevere,
Nor hardships great nor hidden dangers fear.

Life hath ne'er been to me a field of flowers,
The world hath ne'er allured me to its bowers;
I find the thorn more quickly than the rose;
Seldom for me the buds their sweets disclose.

Sometimes they're touched by the untimely frost,
Sometimes by blight or hidden worm they're lost;
But though I mourn, my sorrow I restrain :
God loveth those to whom He giveth pain.

Renounce the world, its pomp, its gilded show,
And seek the well-springs of thy life to know ;
Its turbid waters will become more pure
When Sin and Folly's whirl no longer lure.

Renounce the world ! It yields nor peace nor joy,
Nor aught of happiness without alloy;
Strive for the crown the humblest Christian wins,
And pray forgiveness for thy many sins.

For thee my heart will frequent plead in prayer;
Though strong its love, it shall not prove a snare :
I know thy power, yet hold myself to be
Able to triumph o'er the world and thee.

SONG OF THE FORSAKEN.

WHEN the flowers were in bloom
Justly proud our homestead stood,
Buried in the shadows cool
Of the silver maple wood ;

And the locust's lovely plumes,
And the woodbines o'er the door,
And a wealth of leaf and bloom
Threw their shadows on the floor.

When the flowers were in bloom—
Never flowers half so fair
As those blossoms of my youth,
Raining fragrance on the air—

Never sward so emerald green
As the lawn that spread around—
Never roses half so fair
Shed their petals on the ground.

Ah, the roses! where are they?
Doth the summer bring them still,
Though the roses of my life
Never more shall bloom at will?

Is the woodbine's breath as sweet
Now as in the days of old?
Bloom the violets in the turf
And the crocus buds of gold?

Roses come and roses go,
Summer's warmth and winter's snow;
But no blossoms for her life
Who is neither maid nor wife!

THE APPROACH.

'It is sweet, gentle Death.'
SINTRAM AND HIS COMPANIONS.

As I watch the moments go
My life runneth very low,
  Very near seems Death.
If he reachèd out his hand
From the place where he doth stand,
  He could stop my breath.

This is not the spectral form
Come to chill my pulses warm,
  And to seal my sight ;
This is not the phantom grim
That I fancied Death had been :
  'Tis a form of light.

Tales they told me long ago ;
Now I see they are not so,
  For his mien so fair :
In his arms I have not lain,
But I know that woe and pain
  Cannot reach me there.

ANSWER

TO THE HYMN

' Why thus longing, thus forever sighing
For the far-off, unattained, and dim,
While the beautiful all round thee lying
Offers up its low perpetual hymn ?'

Know you not that He who planted
   In our hearts this longing dim
Knew the unattained would draw us
   Ever nearer unto Him ?

Though the bee, and bud, and blossom
   Bring us lessons every day,
All in vain their gentle teaching
   If our work we turn away.

They whose lives are ever fruitful
   Are the ones who strive to know,
First, the duties lying near them,
   Next, to live for friend and foe.

Who so poor that hath not round them
  Thrown some rays of joy and light?
Who so lorn, so sad and weary,
  As to always dwell in night?

When the longing falls upon us
  Nothing can its chafings still:
He who made our hearts for loving
  Knows that nought but love can fill.

If the dear eyes are not near us
  For whose glance we thirst alone—
If we may not hear the voices
  That once answered to our own—

Is it sin to weep in silence
  (Wearing to the world a mask)
E'en while working for the Master
  Who apportions every task?

Though the fickle crowd applaud us,
  Though we find unsought renown,
We must bear our earthly crosses
  Till we win our heavenly crown.

If the fickle crowd breathes hatred,
    If it tears our laurels down,
'Tis not given to the worthless
    To take up the martyr's crown.

They who live to work for others
    Have not learned to live in vain ;
They who share the griefs of others
    Learn to lighten their own pain ;

And in listening to the teachings
    Of fair Nature's chanted hymn
Thus the restless yearning draws them
    Ever nearer unto Him.

LETTERS.

IN dewy shades the violet grows,
   Shedding its perfume sweet ;
The passer-by with careless step
   Treads it beneath his feet.
But still its incense to the air
   With lavish waste is spread ;
Bruised though it be, its sweetness rests
   Until the flower is dead.

But if some thoughtless hand should pluck
   The flower from its stem,
And hold it to the sun's hot rays,
   Where is its sweetness then ?
So with the words of love that flow
   In written converse sweet—
If taken from their sacred shade
   The eyes of all to greet ;
For ever flown their magic spell,
   No art can e'er recall
The heart's perfume that in them lies
   Which was not shed for all.

IT MIGHT HAVE BEEN.

RIGI wrapped in purple shadows,
   Pilatus bathed in dusky gold,
All the placid lake between them,
   And the peaks of mountains bold,
In the amber light of sunset
   Like a dream of heaven lay ;
But my heart was steeped in sadness,
   For its heaven was far away.

No more in the living present,
   But within the buried past,
Will my thoughts for ever wander,
   Like the ghosts in Hades cast—
Restless spirits that are tortured
   By the joys they cannot win,
Or the anguish that is written
   In these words : ' *It might have been.*'

LUCERNE.

GRIEF, CONSCIENCE, AND FAITH.

WITH Grief I stood one day so face to face
That every lineament my eyes could trace ;
Her cheeks were whiter than the drifting snow
Whereon no sunbeam throws a radiant glow.
She laid her marble hand upon my breast.
Good heart ! as fades the sunshine in the west,
Thereat the colours of my life grew pale,
And every joy and pleasure straight did fail.
'Ah, Grief !' I cried, 'what doest thou with me ?
For Christ's dear sake, O Grief! I pray thee, flee.'
' Ah ! but for Christ's dear sake I came,' she cried,
' To lead thee, wanderer, to thy Saviour's side.'
And so my bruised and bleeding heart we bore,
And laid the offering at the Saviour's door.

Then Conscience said, ' Is this a gift for Christ ?
The heart which friends have careless thrown
     aside,
Wounded and pierced, with earthly passions dyed,
All bruised and torn—is this a gift for Christ ? '

And trembling, I shrank back in mortal fear,
And answered, ' Nay, oh nay ; yet leave it here ;
For Christ Himself was once by friends betrayed,
And I will adjuration make,' I said.
' For pity's sake, though great indeed my sin
In loving creature more than loving Him,—
For pity's sake, He yet may hear my cry,
And stoop to lift me when He passeth by.'
Then Faith cried out, ' Oh ye of little trust,
Christ loves you most when humbled in the dust.'

THE COUNTRY.

MY heart is light within me
  When the days are bright and long,
And my soul breathes forth its music
  As the bird trills forth its song.

My heart is light within me,
  For I love the woodland air,
And in these peaceful pine groves
  I have no thought of care.

All nature lies around me,
  Serene and calm and still ;
The blue sky bends above me
  To meet the arching hill.

And all amidst the space so wide,
  No human form I see
To break the holy solitude
  Of valley, hill, and lea.

And yet I never feel alone,
　Nor weary of the scene :
For far more dear than city spires
　Are these grand trees of green.

Bright orioles flash from bough to bough ;
　Their joyous notes they pour,
Sweet strains of gushing melody
　That drown the waters' roar.

For down in yonder dark ravine
　There falls a silvery stream ;
Tossing around the mossy rocks,
　Wild as a poet's dream.

Fair field flowers lift their fragile heads
　Where'er the eye doth fall ;
Amid the waving wheat and rye
　I see the poppies tall ;

Like coals of fire in embers pale
　Their brilliant blossoms glow ;
And drifting all along the lanes
　The daisies spread their snow.

Ah! not with birds and brooks and flowers
　Could I e'er feel alone ;
For always in wild Nature's haunts
　My sweetest joys are known.

And to our God, who made this earth
　So beautiful and fair,
My heart sends up its offering
　Of ceaseless praise and prayer.

HOME.

OH peaceful home! how sweet within thy walls
   To watch the dying of the golden day,
Knowing that soon unto thy cheerful halls
   A loved one's smile will shed a brighter ray!
How fondly do I watch the changeful skies,
   Fading from crimson to the violet's hue,
And long for eve, that I may meet his eyes,
   Which, like the stars, shine steadily and true!
Oh happy home! how much with pleasure fraught
   Are all the changing scenes thou bring'st to me!
How much of joy that I had never thought
   Could in this world of disappointment be!
Most gladly do I bring unto thy shrine
   The wild desires, the gilded hopes, of youth ;
No more for dreamy visions shall I pine,
   Sure of thy boundless and thy changeless truth.

Oh blissful home! what wonder that I sigh
   Lest some rude blow destroy these scenes so fair,
And Love, affrighted, spread her wings and fly,
   And leave me brooding o'er my own despair ?

With trembling hand I seek to draw the veil
    Which hides the future from my earnest gaze ;
But, like a far and fast receding sail,
    Pale shadows glide into the distant maze.
Oh earthly home ! my spirit feels how frail
    Are all the ties which bind it here to thee—
How much of sorrow in this tearful vale !
    How much of storm upon life's treacherous sea !
And if the bark which we have launched with care
    Before these angry storms be wildly driven,
Oh grant, my God, the fragile wreck may bear
    Its precious freight to the blest *home of Heaven.*

GRAND-CHILDREN.

I HASTEN to my hallowed room
　　When twilight shadows fall,
Where faces that I love the best
　　Look on me from the wall.

But not for their dear smiles alone,
　　In silent welcome sweet ;
It is to listen to the sound
　　Of pattering little feet.

They gladden but a neighbour's home,
　　Yet through the kindly wall
The happy sound comes unto me,
　　I hear each soft footfall.

And here I sit and close my eyes,
　　And think how, o'er the sea,
Some little feet are pattering now,
　　So very dear to me.

Oh, far across the stormy sea,
And far beyond the main—
So far my heart doth often ask,
Shall we e'er meet again ?

And then the tears fall thick and fast ;
My heart is like to break ;
I long to reach the little ones
In my fond arms to take.

. Oh, precious pets beyond the wall,
Within the home you bless
No one looks on a vacant seat,
None miss a lost caress.

But ever, as the days go by
And twilight shadows fall,
The patter of your little feet
Such memories recall,

That often I look wistfully
To the Immortal shore,
Where tears and sorrows never come,
And partings are no more.

MAUD.

To what shall I liken matchless Maud ?
The queen of flowers that poets laud
      Cannot with her compare ;
No lily drooping in valley low
Where only purest of lilies grow
      Was ever half so fair.

Eyes that would shame the stars of night,
So pure their flashing depth of light,
      Yet shy as wild gazelle's ;
Lips of as rich and bright a dye
As carmine fields in Orient sky
      When chime the vesper bells ;

Cheeks of as rare a curve and mould
As ever shaped by sculptor old
      In palmiest days, I ween ;
And waves of silken, sunny hair
Shading the brow divinely fair
      Of our sweet household queen —

All these are hers ; and, ah ! we fear
Such charms, increasing every year,
    A dangerous dower will be.
God shield our little Maud from ill
Shall be our prayer, as ever, till
    We've crossed life's changeful sea.

THE MESSAGE.

' I have a presentiment of approaching evil.'
LETTER.

'TWAS yester eve I felt the same ;
It is no longer so,
For rays of hope illume my heart,
And shed within their glow.
Then scatter to the wind your fears,
And bid your heart be strong ;
You hold your fate within your hands :
Make not the right seem wrong.

Thy message, Heaven-sent to-day
In answer to my prayer,
Has reassured my boding soul,
And lifted all its care.
Henceforth I'll wait with patient trust :
' *Whatever is, is right;*'
I will not murmur at His will
Though clouds shut out the light.

And may He fill your life with joy,
  And round with love your days ;
Then, though our paths be far apart,
  Still will I render praise.
Now give unto the winds your fears,
  And bid your heart be strong ;
You hold your fate within your hands :
  Make not the right seem wrong.

COMPENSATION.

'Thou shalt be hidden from the scourge of the tongue.'

JOB V. 21.

FORGET not, Lord, Thy promises
　To those who trust in Thee ;
Close not Thy ears unto their cries,
　Nor from their presence flee.

For Thou art mighty in Thy strength,
　And we are weak and frail ;
To combat evil without Thee
　What would our powers avail ?

O Lord, how long must we endure,
　How long the scourge abide,
Before Thy arms shall fold us round,
　Thy love our sorrows hide ?

We plead the promises of old,
　Weary and faint we cry ;
Withhold not, Lord, thy sheltering grace
　When unto Thee we fly.

' Mortal! hope not while here on earth
  God's chastening rod to flee ;
Rather lift up thy heart in praise
  That *thus* He chasteneth thee.

' Not with fierce trials born of shame,
  Nor sorrows steeped in sin,
Hast thou to walk thy pilgrimage,
  His courts to enter in.

' He giveth thee thy every wish,
  Reserving *only one*—
To draw thee always near to Him,
  And to His Saviour Son.'

The still, small Voice was heard no more,
  But round me and above
God's holy angels seemed to float,
  And all was peace and love.

SYMPATHY.

'For a loving heart to lack sympathy is worse than pain.'
REV. F. W. ROBERTSON.

WHY should we fly to human aid
    To tell our tales of woe,
When God's just ear is ever lent
    Unto our cries below?

What solace can it give like His?
    What strength whereon to rest
Like that we find at His dear feet
    When by our griefs opprest?

Teach me, my God, to turn to Thee
    Whenever storms shall lower,
Remembering how weak is man,
    How strong Thy gracious power.

My every grief at Thy dear feet,
    My every care, I'll leave;
Thy love shall heal each bleeding wound;—
    I shall no longer grieve.

HOW LONG?

How long, O Lord, how long?
  My weary soul makes plaint;
How long, Lord, wilt Thou hold
  Thy arms from those who faint?

My cause is Thine, O God!
  For justice, truth, and right
I looked to Thee for help,
  And trusted in Thy might.

I know that not in vain
  I place my hope in Thee,
That when Thy time is ripe
  Sure is my victory.

How long, O Lord, how long?
  My weary soul makes plaint;
Eternal truth and justice reign:
  Let not my heart grow faint.

A MEMORY OF THE NILE.

A steamer with the American flag passed our dahabeah, January 31, 1866, the passengers singing, 'Rally round the flag, boys.'

A DAY of calm : our sails were down ;
The boatmen idly rowed ;
An azure sky without a cloud :
The Nile scarce rippling flowed.

The palm groves stood against the sky,
And not a leaf was stirred ;
The camels grazed amidst the fields,
The shepherd watched his herd.

Women, with flashing Orient eyes,
And garments flowing free,
Paused with their water jars erect
The Frank's pale face to see.

Their turbaned lords reclined at ease
   In groups along the shore;
Each scene a picture to our eyes,
   The day thus onward wore.

When, lo! a steamer speeding past
   With Stars and Stripes on high!
Our hearts beat fast, our pulses thrill,
   Tears start from every eye.

The dear old flag!   So far from home,
   What memories it brings!
Straightway across the distant seas
   Our fancies spread their wings.

We seem to hear the bugle strains
   Of pealing battle hymns,
Which nerved our hearts to earnest work
   And kindled statesmen's themes.

We seem to hear—Oh no, for now,
   Swelling upon the air,
The very strains that fancy brought
   The morning wind doth bear.

O God! if thus the heart can leap,
  If thus the soul can thrill,
While denizens of earth we roam
  Where pleasure leads at will,

What must the life celestial bring
  When, on that heav'nly shore,
We see the dearest loved on earth
  Whom Thou didst call before,

And hear their voices on the air,
  Blent with the seraphs' song,
In strains of welcome unto those
  Who join their holy throng?

Eye hath not seen nor ear hath heard
  The joys that crown the blest,
For never unto mortal heart
  The least hath been confest.

But if, when in a foreign land
  Our wandering footsteps roam,
Our bodies scarce our souls contain
  When rings some lay of home,

Shall we not guess the finer joy
  Unto the spirit born
When from the night of death it soars
  To reach the heavenly morn ?

THE DYING WIFE.

' For death itself I did not fear ;
'Tis love that makes the pain.'—E. B. B.

OPEN the casement wide and give me air,
　And let me look once more upon the sky,
Once more upon my earthly home so fair,
　Once more before I die.

How gently doth the south wind fan my brow,
　Kissing the tresses damp with death's cold dew
How sweet the clustering flowers on yon green
　　bough !
　The far-off heaven how blue !

More beautiful to me the earth doth seem,
　Now that I know the parting hour is near,
More terrible the sleep without one dream,
　The grave more dark and drear.

Clasp close the hand that hath not strength to
   press ;
Kiss, kiss the lips that soon will be so cold ;
Say when I'm gone you will not love me less
   Than in the days of old.

Beloved, it is a bitter thing to die,
   To feel the pulse grow weak while love is strong,
To know that dim and dimmer grows the eye
   That watched thy smile so long.

Ah ! earth hath been to me too much like heaven,
   Thy love hath made me prize my life too well ;
But earthly treasures are but lent, not given,
   As thy fond tears will tell.

Then let me die. I would not live to see
   Thy smile wax less, faint and more faint thy
      tone ;
Life would be worse than death, dear love, to me,
   If thou, my life, wert gone.

     *   *   *   *   *   *   *

Ah, there is neither death nor sorrow there,
   And God is love ; and love to us is given
To make our earthly life more passing fair,
   And more of bliss our heaven.

No more thy grieving, mournful plaint
  Would echo in my breast,
But tones of joy would ever chant
  My troubled thoughts to rest.

Angels stoop low to bear thee up ;
  Resigned unto their sway,
Their wings shall cleave the arching blue
  As cleaves the mid-sun's ray.

Before the throne where seraphs bow,
  Beside the waters still,
And through the pastures fresh and green,
  Thou'lt walk with them at will.

Ah ! blest be God that hope and love
  And faith to us are given,
Angels to lift our souls from earth
  And ope the gates of heaven.

IN MEMORIAM.

THE MIDNIGHT VIGIL.

THE winds are holding carnival to-night,
  Driving their chariot clouds across the sky ;
Weird sounds are borne upon the troubled air
  As troop by troop the pale hosts hurry by.

They waken superstitions of my youth
  Which years ago I thought were lulled to rest,
When Reason took them in her matron arms
  And rocked them sleeping on her matron breast.

But now these sobs, once more upon the night,
  Fall as before in days so long ago ;
I seem to hear low voices murmur by
  In waves of sound as tides that ebb and flow ;

Are the pale spirits of the dead now loose,
  Calling for others their pale ranks to swell ?
Oh, pass us by within this loving home—
  Come not anear us with such purpose fell !

I keep my vigils by a sleeping form ;
  The tears fall ever from my watching eyes.
O God, in mercy grant he may be spared !
  Who could replace him in his counsels wise ?

Who could replace him in his tender love ?
  Who the great void could ever, ever fill ?
Ah, cease thy questionings, fond and feeble heart,
  And learn to wait upon God's holy will.

The wind in peaceful murmurs dies away ;
  A sacramental silence fills the air ;
The spirits of the just are round about,
  And God, in whom I trust, is everywhere.

December 1859.

AFTER THE VIGIL.

THEY told me time would deaden grief;
   And so I sat with folded hands,
And waited for the slow relief,
   And watched the hour-glass' glittering sands.

The days went by I knew not how;
   I only knew he was not here;
Morning and night were all the same,
   Morning and night alike were drear.

One thought I mused on o'er and o'er:
   'If love survives the grave,' I said,
'He will come back to us again;
   They cannot keep him with the dead.

' His every thought was for our weal;
   Can he so soon forget us there
As any happiness to know
   While our sharp cries still cleave the air?'

Then came thick clouds across my brain ;
　My faith and trust were lost in gloom ;
‘ This is the end of man ! ’ I cried ;
　‘ All that once loved lies in the tomb ! ’

Appalling thought !　My reason reeled ;
　Life seemed to me a cruel jest ;
I mourned the hour that gave me birth,
　And called upon the grave for rest.

God answered not my erring prayer,
　But gently took me by the hand,
And led me to the house of want,
　And whispered there His wise command :—

Go feed the hungry, bind the bruised,
　Speak to the dying words of cheer ;
So shalt thou feel within thy heart
　Thy heaven begun, though wandering here.

‘ So shalt thou feel his spirit still
　Ever in ministry with thine ;
Mortal, he is not lost to thee :
　He waits beyond the bounds of time.’

DEATH.

O WONDROUS sphinx ! within thy marble breast
    What undreamed secrets lie concealed !
Hast thou no pity for my wild unrest—
    My maddening longing for the unrevealed ?

As soon might I expect the stones to melt
    Beneath the vernal April's frequent rain ;
As soon might I expect thou wouldst relent,
    And give unto my arms my dead again.

' Blind on the rocks,' I stand, and stretch my hands;
    Wearied and faint, unto my God I cry ;
Oh ! show to me these mysteries of Death,
    Even if them to learn I too must die.

The days pass on. He does not heed my prayer ;
    He still has work on earth for me begun ;
Ah, wondrous sphinx ! my lips will one day wear
    Thy smile of peace when all my work is done.

K

Then shall my soul escape these bonds of clay,
  Soaring through space to solve thy secrets old ;
Then shall my dead be given back to me ;
  Then shall the wisdom of my God unfold.

ISABEL.

'And Jesus called a little child to Him.'—MATT. xviii. 2.

WHERE have they led our little Bell,
　The firstling of the fold,
Who was rocked to rest
On her mother's breast
　So tenderly of old?

Where have they led our little Bell?
　Have they left her with the dead?
We miss the pure grace
Of her fair young face;
　Where was the sweet child led?

Down in the churchyard drear and lone,
　Was Isabel left there?
With marble cold cheek,
And hands folded meek,
　Like those of a saint at prayer?

K 2

No, not the graveyard drear and lone
   Holdeth our little Bell.
God opened His gate,
And the royal state
   Of her glory who shall tell?

The angels called her all the day,
   Our dear Lord led her in.
Why should we so weep,
When through gates of sleep
   A sweet child passeth from sin?

1856.

MEMORIES.

AGAIN I stand beside thy grave, my friend,
  Striving in vain to check these flowing tears;
Again above this emerald mound I bend,
  Recalling all our love in childhood's years.

Thy blue eyes, radiant with the spirit's light,
  Again beam on me as in days of yore,
Thy chestnut hair, thy brow so marble white,
  The tender smiles thy sweet lips ever wore.

Again I walk thy lovely form beside;
  Hand clasped in hand, we rove from dale to dale,
And in the shade where flows the crystal tide
  We wreathe the ivy and the lilies pale.

'Tis but a dream; the cypress tree doth wave
  Its gloomy branches o'er thy cherished form,
And moaning night winds whisper round thy grave
  When through these dark pines sweeps the weep-
    ing storm.

Still grow the lilies in yon meadow green,
  Still flows the streamlet o'er the silver sand ;
There's nought to miss from this fair woodland
    scene,
  But the soft pressure of thy clasping hand.

And thou, our fairest lily of the vale,
  Hast faded, wilted, ceased, alas ! to bloom ;
Summer's soft breath can never aught avail
  To raise our flow'ret from the turf-spanned tomb.

But, O my God ! I thank Thee for the faith
  Which to my heart in mercy hath been given ;
For while I mourn a voice within me saith,
  ' Thy lily blooms more beautiful in heaven.'

A DIRGE.

STAINLESS lilies of the vale,
Fragile lilies, pure and pale,
　　Slowly toll your snowy bells!
Hear ye not a mournful tale
In the zephyr's dying wail
　　As it murmurs through the dells?

Meadow violets, meek and low,
White as any flake of snow,
　　Closer bow your heads to earth!
Do you feel no pang, no throe,
Is there no sign by which you know
　　A mortal's heavenly birth?

Song-birds by that forest side
Where the rippling waters glide,
　　Breathe a slower, sadder strain!
For our hearts send up a plaint
Through our voices low and faint,
　　And she answers not again.

Summer roses gemmed with dew,
Clouds that float o'er heaven's blue,
    All things pure and frail and fair,
Bring some offering to the grave
Where the dark pines nightly wave,
    For our loveliest sleepeth there.

AN ANNIVERSARY.

'The loveliest spot on earth.'

In hallowed silence let me keep this day
  Sacred to one whose home was erstwhile here,
Who hath escaped her pinioned bonds of clay,
  And with the angels roves from sphere to sphere.
We know that sorrow cannot reach her there ;
  We do not wish her back where tears are shed.
Within those regions gloriously fair
  Mysterious joys attend our sainted dead ;
The deepest bliss that earth can e'er bestow
  Hides wearing griefs too oft beneath it all ;
But in those realms no touch of care nor woe
  Upon the pure and ransomed spirit falls.
     *   *   *   *   *   *   *
Only one year ago her home was here,
  And every bud and flower bloomed for her.
She watched the sails that glided far and near,
  The crested tide wooing the rocky shore,

The angel clouds that beckoned her away,
  And all but one short year ago to-day.
How patiently she bore the rod of pain,
  Yet plead for life because it was so dear!
Oh, suffering one, who now within the veil
  Dost see thy Father's wisdom vast and clear,
Could we but know the glories of thy state,
  How should we long to share them there with
    thee!
How would our restless souls scarce deign to wait
  The longed-for hour when Death shall set us free!
Canst thou not bend thy pitying eyes from heaven,
  Filled with their mother-smile of tenderest love,
As shine the distant, holy stars of even,
  From the deep richness of the realms above?

No; ask it not.   He knoweth what is best
Whose joys no eye hath seen nor tongue confest.

NEWPORT, *July* 13, 1868.

A TRIBUTE.

 St. John's Church, Wilmington, Delaware,

Founded by Alexis I. du Pont.

NEVER of dust beneath did sculptured tomb
So eloquently speak as this grey spire
Of thee, O labourer without hire, whose day
Closed with the noon, thy Master calling thee
Straight from the field, before thy work was done,
To rest with Him above.   Before thy work
Was done ?   We dare not say of thee, whose life
Was filled to overflowing with good deeds—
Who crowded labours in the noon-tide hour
So great as this—that aught was left undone.
No.   Blessed be He who set thee to thy task,
And when the hours of servitude were o'er
Redeemed the promise of our Christ, and called
Thee home to glories of thy heritage.
        *   *   *   *   *   *   *
These massive walls defy the hand of Time ;

Long years shall pass and find them still secure ;
Green creeping vines will clamber o'er thy sides
And interlace their sprays.   The passers-by
Will feel with quickening hearts thy untold worth;
And so to children's children will thy name
Go down, kindling to deeds of love men still
Unborn and scattering seeds for harvest-time.

AN AUTUMN SUNSET.

THESE amber clouds of autumn skies,
  Like islands of the blest,
Float on to my enraptured eyes
  Across the radiant west.
With crimson tints the saffron blends,
  Dark purple streaks the sky,
And snow-white masses floating up
  Like sails go gliding by.
The sun has vanished from my sight
  The twilight gathers round;
She casts the banners of the night
  Athwart the vestured ground :
And all the earth is calm and still;
  No sound falls on the ear
Save the low murmur of the stream
  That winds along the mere;
And down, far down, the deep ravine
  Some insect's plaintive cry,

And now and then a wild bird's call
  As flocks go swooping by.
Ah! in the silence of this hour
  How fast the memories throng!
While the tears will rise unbidden
  Although the heart be strong—
Tears which but one short twelvemonth since
  We little thought to shed,
For loving eyes smiled on us then
  That now are with the dead.
We miss the pressure of her hand,
  Her fond and gentle tone,
And wheresoe'er we turn our eyes
  We miss the love-light flown.
Oh, never can this earth put on
  The brightness erst it wore,
Nor autumn winds nor autumn skies
  The glories once they bore.

1851.

A PSALM OF THANKSGIVING.

How can I thank Thee as I would,
  O God! my God of grace!
Who from behind the gloom of death
  Reveal'st Thy smiling face?

How can I thank Thee as I would,
  O God! my God of love!
That Thou hast drawn those weary feet
  To rest in realms above?

How can I thank Thee as I would,
  O God! my God of peace!
That Thou didst send Thy messenger
  With painless, swift release?

I cannot thank Thee as I would,
  But make my life to be .
A ceaseless offering of praise
  For ever, Lord, to Thee!

April 3, 1876.

'BABY ERNALD.'

O ACHING hearts, hold fast your pain !
O eyes that weep, your tears restrain !
The spirit flown comes not again.

Close the fringed lids to dreamless rest;
Fold the sweet hands upon the breast:
God ever knoweth what is best.

Not for our lost these tears that flow :
For us the bitter, bitter woe ;
For him the bliss that angels know.

For us, we bear the anguished pain;
While for *our lost* we look in vain,
Through blinding tears that fall like rain.

———

Father ! we know Thy pitying care !
Help us our aching hearts to bear !

1876.

'*NOT LOST, BUT GONE BEFORE.*'

> ' Ah, Christ, that it were possible
> For one short hour to see
> The souls we loved, that they might tell us
> What and where they be.'
>
> TENNYSON.

' O MY lost one ! precious lost one !
How my heart cries out for thee,
Across the sullen waters
Of death's dark and silent sea !
Day by day I wait an answer,
But no answer comes to me.'

While she listened—vainly listened—
For some sound, though faint as sighs
Straight before her, slowly gliding,
Sailed two glistening dragon-flies
Bringing her the longed-for message
As if tidings from the skies ;

L

For there flashed o'er memory's tablets
  A quick gleam from sudden rays,
Bringing back a German fable
  She had read in happier days,
Full of heavenly inspiration
  As a poet's worthiest lays.

Now the fable as narrated
  I shall here essay to tell,
With the hope that it may lighten
  Griefs like hers, and break the spell,
When in doubt some mourner questions,
  'With my lost ones is it well?'

FABLE OF THE DRAGON-FLY GRUBS.

There was a dark and sedgy pool,
  Where plants grew side by side;
Their roots were fast in mire below,
  Their tops swayed with the tide.

And here, low down on slimy bed,
  Some water creatures crept,
And thought their world a paradise,
  And groped, and ate, and slept.

No care disturbed their life's content,
 Save when some comrade dear
Climbed up a plant to fields of air,
 In them to disappear.

Then gathered they around the case
 Which once contained their kind ;
In solemn conclave sought of each
 The mystery to find.

' How can it be that he exists
 When this is thrown aside ?
Robbed of the form he once possessed,
 Where does he now abide ? '

Then said the eldest of them all,
 ' My turn will come to go,
And I shall find some way to tell
 What each one longs to know.'

The days passed on, and brought at last
 The hour he knew was near ;
And all his kinsfolk gathered round
 His promised words to hear.

He reached the top, he passed the edge
  Where stretched the ether plane ;
The case fell back, its inmate gone ;
  His comrades wait in vain.

No sound they heard, no sight they saw,
  Yet, flashing in the air,
Were iridescent wings of light
  Above them everywhere.

And he, the latest born of all,
  Close-skimmed the water's edge,
Peering far down the murky depths
  Amidst the swaying sedge.

He saw the groping forms below,
  The wistful glances sent,
As they looked upward from their home,
  To gain some tidings bent.

But all in vain he strove to tell,
  The mystery was o'er :
They cannot hear who grope in fear,
  '*Not lost, but gone before.*'

' Not my lost one ! ' said the mourner:
' Now I know thou waitest me
Beyond the brightening waters
Of death's solemn, silent sea ;
And I wait the welcome message
Which will call me unto thee ! '

STORIES FOR CHILDREN.

'KATIE DID:' A GOSSIP'S TALE.

Miss Magpie speaks.

'A GOOD MORNING, Madame Locust!
  Pray, have you heard the tale
About Miss Katie Green, the belle,
  Who lives in yonder vale?'

Mrs. Locust answers.

'Ah! no, indeed, Miss Maggie P.;
  I've not been out, you know;
And living up four pairs of stairs,
  I don't hear much below.
I hope the proud and pretty Kate
  Has not disgraced her name;
Her family are all well-bred,
  For from good blood they came.'

Miss Magpie.

'Well, Madame Locust, pride, you know,
  Is very unbecoming;

But though Kate Green's exceeding proud,
 She always was a-roaming,
And they do say she's very fast,
 And very wilful too;
And though I'm not at all a prude,
 Some things I'd never do.
And now they say she has eloped,
 With her own cousin too.
I don't believe all that I hear,
 But this I know is true,
For as I passed her mother's house
 I stopped beside the door,
And heard her sobbing " Katie did ;"
 I could not well hear more.'

Mrs. Locust.

' Why, that's a song they always sing
 When all the world is still :
I'm sure you must have heard them
 From every dale and hill.
I listen almost every night
 When in their homes they're hid,
Singing always the selfsame tune :
 The words are " Katie did."

I would not, then, repeat the tale,
  My friend, if I were you,
Until you have some better proof
  Of knowing it is true.'

The busy day passed round again,
  And evening, as before,
Found gossiping Miss Magpie
  At Neighbour Locust's door.

Miss Magpie.

'That story, Madame Locust,
  Is true as true can be;
For what's before one's own eyes
  One cannot help but see.
Dame Hornet lives just opposite
  Miss Katie's mother's door,
And I stepped in this afternoon:
  I never called before.
They're not counted in our set,
  Nor are they 'in the swim,'
But one must be agreeable
  When news one seeks to win.
So I found she knew her neighbours,
  And she talked for full an hour

About the Greens—how rich they were,
And how they built a bower
Of emerald leaves and coral buds
For Katie's use alone,
And to reward their kindness fond
The wanton thing has flown.
And no one knows where she has gone.
Her mother wept all day;
And when Mrs. Hornet asked her,
One word she would not say.'

Mrs. Locust.

' Stop, stop, my friend! you talk too fast.
I know where Kate has gone.
Look through my vine-clad window,
And o'er yon verdant lawn.
You see that dwelling rich and chaste,
As fair as e'er was seen?
That is the home of Katie now:
Her name is *Mrs.* Green.
Her mother came around to-day
To sit a while with me;
And when I found she felt so lone,
I made her stay to tea.

Her Katie did not run away;
  She rode like any queen:
Two snow-white doves her coursers were,
  Her carriage gold and green,
A present from her loving lord
  Upon her bridal day.
Oh! that he is her cousin dear
  I quite forgot to say.
'Twas Katie's wish, her mother said,
  To have it kept so still;
There were no guests besides the Greens
  And Mrs. Whippoorwill.
But though her mother mourns her loss,
  I saw her eyes' deep light,
Which flashed so proudly when she told
  The splendours of that night—
The costly gifts his friends had brought
  To lavish on the bride;
And though she spoke with faltering tones,
  I saw her heartfelt pride.
So take a warning, Maggie Pye:
  With gossips don't be seen;
And if you hear some idle tale
  Remember Katie Green.

And don't give ear to slanders vile,
   Much less the words repeat,
Or you will live to be despised
   And scorned by those you meet.'

COWARDS.

HAROLD asks a story. What shall it be?
Of beautiful lands beyond the broad sea?
Or of fairies and gnomes in forests deep?
Or of soldiers who fight and women who weep?

'Tell me *all*, grandmamma—tell *all* to me;
Fairies and gnomes and lands beyond the sea.
First tell me, please, of the soldiers who fight;
If wrong for us boys, for men is it right?'

And Carl, standing by, opens wide his eyes,
Large, lovely and calm, and full of surprise:
'Can I fight, grandma, when I am a man?
Because I will wait until then, if I can.

'I would like to strike when Ulla looks grum
And sends me to bed for breaking my drum,
But I am so small and so short, you know,
I cannot reach up to give her a blow.'

' Oh, naughty Carl Diedrick! do you not know
They're cowards who strike a woman a blow?'
Cries Harold, looking severe as he can:
' But never a soldier, and never a man.'

DOGGEREL.

THREE little children waiting in a row,
Three little ponies saddled ' for to go,'
Three big chimney-sweeps stalking through the
town,
The three frightened children all tumble down.

Three little ponies scampering one side,
Three little children much terrified ;
Three stalking chimney-sweeps full of delight,
Having occasioned the terrible fright.

Ten big Prussians going to the field,
Two little Frenchmen that will not yield ;
One mitrailleuse pouring out its fire,
Ten big Prussians marching on in ire.

Two little Frenchmen running like mad ;
The mitrailleuse which the Frenchmen had
Turned by the Prussians to fire on their foe ;
The two little Frenchmen don't know where to go.

Three big chimney-sweeps stalk all the night,
Trying to give other children a fright ;
Ten big Prussians following up their foe,
Two little Frenchmen still ' on the go.'

Three little ponies at a stable door,
Two little Frenchmen dying in their gore ;
Ten big Prussians flying to their king,
Who think they've done a wonderful thing.

Moral.

Though chimney-sweeps and bullies may some-
    times prevail,
We have not yet come to the end of the tale ;
The weak will grow strong, and the children some day
Will get to be men, and will go their own way.

When equal the numbers, a combat brings fame
To the victor who keeps untarnished his name.
Boys are bullies who press their much weaker foes,
And when they are fallen continue their blows.

Remember this, boys, when you've grown to be
    men—
Reinhold, Carl Clarence, and little Eugène ;
And if you should chance to have ever a foe,
When he is fallen don't strike him a blow.

THE BIRDS' NEST.

A STORY FOR ERIC.

' OH, mamma, I have seen the home
    Of the robin and the wren ;
It was the dearest, sweetest spot
    In all the wooded glen.

' The leaves were thickly hung around ;
    You could not see the sky ;
And there, upon the shadiest bough,
    They'd hung their nests so high.

' I could not reach, for all I tried
    And stood upon my toes,
And thought to coax the black-eyed birds
    By holding up my rose.

' It frightened them ; they left their nests,
    And swiftly flew away ;
I trembled for the little birds,
    And wanted them to stay.

' Then from behind a laurel bush
  I watched with eager view,
While, hopping back from bough to bough,
  The birdies' mammas flew.

' They snugged up to their little ones,
  And then I ran away ;
But may I not go back again
  To see their nests some day ? '

So little Edla asked mamma,
  And mamma said, ' My dear,
How would you like if giants came
  Within our cottage here ?

' And if they frightened me away,
  How would you feel to see
The awful creatures standing near—
  As near as near could be ? '

Then Edla shook her little head,
  With curls of sunny gold ;
And quickly answering, Edla said,
  ' The half could not be told

' Of all the fear that I should feel.
Even for birds 'tis true :
" Do unto others as you would
That others do to you." '

THE LITTLE TRUANT.

[ILLUSTRATION OF A PICTURE.]

' WHERE hast thou been, thou beautiful child?
Wandering o'er hillsides, through woodlands wild,
Frightening the birds from the forest spray,
And gathering flowers by the shaded way?
Why art thou standing in thoughtful mood?
Is the brook too wanton, the breeze too rude?
Or art thou wearied with idle play—
Wearied with rambling all the day?'

' Afar through the vales where fountains flow,
And over the hills where violets grow,
And down in the meadows wide and green,
Where the lily droops its head unseen,
There have I wandered this lovely day
With the humming bees and the birds to play.

' I fear to go to my mother mild;
I know she has missed her truant child,

And, sadly grieved at my absence long,
She'll chide her darling for doing wrong ;
But oh, 'tis beautiful on the lea :
With the birds and flowers I love to be.

' I will take my buds to my mother dear,
And tell her for me she must never fear,
For I love the fresh and the sunny air,
The woodlands wild and the valleys fair ;
And God, who careth for bird and bee,
I am sure will always care for me.'

VOICES OF THE PAST.

MY COUNTRY.

WHAT shall I do for thee, my land,
    In this thy hour of need ?
Thy cry goes up unto the skies,
    And shall I take no heed ?

Shall all my nights be spent in rest,
    And all my days in ease,
While thousands sleep in tented fields
    Beneath the wintry breeze,

And thousands more by silent hearths
    Await the battle-cry ?
The keenest suffering in war
    Comes not to those who die.

O God ! to think of all the woe
    Beneath the mourner's roof,
The days of sickening, sad suspense
    That herald in the truth !

O God! to think of all the tears
That drench this hapless land
From Mississippi's winding course
To broad Atlantic's strand!

Ah! mothers, wives, and sisters fond
Who wait the tidings dread,
I would our country might be saved,
And you still weep no dead.

But did I count as many sons
As did Cornelia bold,
I'd gird myself their weapons on,
And speed them from my fold.

My eyes are full of gathering tears,
But not for those away;
Alas that I've not one to send
To fight our cause to-day!

I'll give my time, my life, my all;
And may the offering be
As worthy of thee, O my land,
As if I died for thee!

January 1864.

'FORWARD, MARCH!'

ON Newbern's bloody battle-ground,
  Bold as a crusade knight,
Our young lieutenant led us on,
  All eager for the fight.

'Forward, my men, my comrades brave!'
  His voice rang loud and clear;
And, charging with our bayonets,
  We followed in the rear.

And, ever foremost, on he pressed;
  Our ranks held firm and true,
Though volley after volley poured,
  And thinned us through and through.

'Well done, my boys! the day is ours!
  Like veterans you've fought!'
Another crash of musketry:
  The day was dearly bought;

For there upon the accursèd soil
   Our young lieutenant lay;
Too brave for even one low moan,
   His life-blood ebbed away.

Loud rang his voice, as clarion clear,
   As when he onward led :
'Forward, my boys! the day is ours!'
   Then fell back with the dead.

And 'Forward!' is our battle-cry,
   Which through the land shall ring
Until the Union is restored
   And Liberty is king.

I.

IN ROME, MAY 1863.

NOT for Italy waking from fetters
Of centuries' pestilent sleep,
Not for Italy arming for freedom,
These tears of compassion I weep;
But my thoughts flow afar from this region,
Afar from its classical lore,
My thoughts flow afar from this region,
Back, back to my own native shore.
I mourn on the banks of the Tiber
For the ills of my own native shore.

O Columbia! fairest of countries,
Must thy valleys, so fruitful and still,
Be shorn, like these plains, of their glory,
And yield to the conqueror's will?
Thy cities be swept of the treasures
By peace and prosperity won,
Whilst the carnage of battle is raging
'Twixt father and brother and son?

O Columbia! fairest of countries,
  Have the days of thy sorrow begun?

The days when the tears of thy orphans
  Shall sprinkle thy green sod like rain,
When countless the wives and the mothers
  Who mourn o'er their wounded and slain;
When the hopes of the nations in darkness,
  Whose eyes turned upon thee for light,
Shall grow faint in thy bitter despairing,
  Shall be lost in the blackness of night?
Alas for the hopes of the nations
  That trusted thy glory and might!

O Rome! in the days of thy glory,
  In the days of thy pomp and thy pride,
When thy legions outnumbered the nations
  Which thou in thy triumph defied,
Didst thou dream of the sad devastation
  That, hurtling o'er hillside and plain,
Should sweep down thy temples and columns
  As low as thy warriors slain?
Didst thou dream of the long night of silence
  That should fall o'er thy beautiful plain?

II.

AT HOME, MAY 1864.

THUS mused I in dark days of sadness
Ere the purpose of God I had seen :
Our country was shattered and falling,
No strength had it whereon to lean.
But now dawns its day of redemption,
The time of its triumph draws nigh ;
No longer a nation of bondsmen
Lift manacled hands to the sky ;
But God in His glory appeareth,
And cleaving the channel of red
These dark hosts, by Him marshalled over,
The fair land of promise shall tread ;
And the eyes of the nations in darkness
Shall *still* turn upon us for light,
As, scaling the pure heights of freedom,
We grow in our grandeur and might.

N

WIDOWED.

[ADMIRAL DU PONT DIED JUNE 30, 1865.]

TRUE to herself, to her heroic heart,
  Resigned she counts the hours that slowly glide,
As when her country called, though loth to part,
  She braved the days that kept him from her side.

Ah! those were times of troubled, wearing fear,
  But through the murderous storms of shot and
    shell
He lived to count his victory complete,
  And meet the homage he had earned so well.

' Waiting for orders,' to his home he sped.
  Ah, God be praised! the orders never came,
And months slipped by in joy and solace rare,
  Save that the land he loved was scourged by
    flame—

Save that unto his judgment and his skill,
   Ripened by rich experience of years,
They paid no heed, but wrought the weaker will,
   While Time made manifest how just his fears ;

How wise and true, counsels that might have saved
   An untold number of most precious lives,
Uncounted sums of treasure to our land,
   And myriad tears of mothers, sisters, wives!

'Waiting for orders !'   Suddenly they came,
   But not to marshal hosts as erst before ;
Not into danger's midst God calls him now,
   But through the portals of His golden door.

His perfect life, rounded with duties filled,
   Closed on him calmly as a summer's day;
No shock of pain, no anguished gaze of love,
   Wrestled in vain to bid his spirit stay.

The scathing flame had cleansed his country free,
   And holy Peace was brooding o'er the land ;
A fitting time for one to pass from earth
   Whose days have left us such a record grand.

But for the anguish of his widowed one
  We may not check unbidden tears that flow;
Comfort her with Thy presence, O our Christ!
  And give her peace such as God's angels know.

OUR HERO.

Ulysses S. Grant.

As some great Sphinx looms up before the sight,
To travellers crossing o'er the Libyan sands,
Calm and majestic in its grand repose
As are the chiselled saints of Christian lands ;
So, in the future, will his name bring up
To those who tread the golden sands of life,
His deeds heroic in our time of need—
His greatness when had closed the days of strife.
And, like that Sphinx with face serene and calm,
Those deeds, this greatness, shall for ever stand,
Kindling the hearts of nations yet unborn—
Thrilling the noble souls of every land !

THE SEASONS.

AN APRIL DAY.

THE April rain falls slowly,
  Like tears that follow sighs,
And fleecy clouds glide lightly
  Over the azure skies;
The soft south wind is wooing
  The pale clematis vine,
Dallying with its tendrils
  As trustingly they twine.

The east a rainbow spanneth,
  Promise of watchful care—
A glowing, gorgeous banner,
  That fairies might prepare
With rays of gold and purple,
  With emeralds' flashing light,
With tints from deep blue sapphires,
  And hearts of rubies bright.

From sward that spreads before me
    The crocus lifts its head,
And pale and starry flowers
    Peep from their winter bed;
And o'er the latticed trellis
    The clinging vine doth creep,
While down amid the mossy turf
    The harebell lies asleep.

I love the gentle April—
    Her soft and balmy sighs;
Her smiles are ofttimes tearful,
    But hope's in her earnest eyes;
Sweet in truth is the lesson
    That grief may learn alway,
For, ever, weeping April
    Is followed by joyous May.

A DAY IN MIDSUMMER.

Lo! from yonder rising upland
　　Springs the dewy-footed Morn,
Sweeping with her waving garments
　　Through the fields of rustling corn.
Through the vale she swiftly glideth,
　　Breathing on the billowy grain,
And, like amber wavelets flowing,
　　See it sparkle o'er the plain.

Now she bends beside the fountain
　　In the deep and dark ravine,
Bathes her lips and sunny forehead,
　　Wreathes her brow with garlands green.
In the grand old woods she wanders,
　　Through the blossoming leafy bowers,
Weaving in a perfumed chaplet
　　Tender buds and sweetest flowers.

To the lightly-dancing streamlet
   Breatheth she sweet notes of glee
As adown the rocks it leapeth,
   Laughing o'er the level lea.
In her eyes you see no traces
   Of the depths of natal gloom
Which her parent, Night, enshrouded,
   As she weeping left his tomb.

Light of heart, she onward hastens,
   Humming o'er the water's tune,
While, upon the hill-tops sleeping,
   Waits her younger sister, Noon.
Morn awakes her with her kisses,
   And the beauty lifts her eyes
On the sunny vales and uplands
   Where the grass enamelled lies.

Flinging back her golden tresses,
   Waving in voluptuous light,
Now the graceful Noon arises,
   Glorious in her sister's sight.
Then the maiden Morn departeth,
   And sweet Noon walks forth alone,
Languishing beside the fountains
   For her lovely sister flown.

Every hour she grows still sadder,
Every hour she mourns in vain,
Till at length the star-crowned Evening
Hastens o'er the lonely plain;
Struck with wonder at the beauty
Even of her fading charms,
Evening bows entranced before her,
And she sleeps within his arms.

AUTUMN SCENES.

AUTUMN is here.   His russet mantle's fold
   Trails over all the woodland groves around,
Scattering bright gems of purple set in gold
   Like drifts of amethysts to the mossy ground.
The katydid has ceased her plaintive tale,
   The whippoorwill has sought a southern zone,
Alone the corn-bird calls along the vale,
   And listens to the hoarse wind's answering tone.

The grass-grown path beside the chestnut wood
   Is nearly hidden by the drifting leaves ;
The plough-boy gleans the nuts where thickest
     strewed,
   Or helps the farmer stack his yellow sheaves ;
The river, murmuring o'er its rocky bed,
   Smiles up as fondly to the forest spray
As if it sought the falling leaves to wed,
   And bear them from their sheltered home away.

The wild flower, shivering on its slender stalk,
    Meets the rude blast, and sways to rise again,
Spreading its petals gay by woodland walk,
    Heedless of drenching dews and beating rain.
Not so its sister plants in garden bowers;
    They droop and die, afraid of winter's cold,
All save the artemisia's clustering flowers,
    The dahlia and the stately marigold.

'Midst all of autumn's ever mournful sounds
    The cricket chirps his never-ceasing lay,
And wild bees, buzzing o'er their daily rounds,
    Hasten to bear their stolen sweets away.
The labourer, plodding homeward from his toil
    O'er fields where gleaners gathered all the day,
Finds a few scattered sheaves upon the soil,
    And with a light heart whistles on his way.

Once in his home, his cheerful wife will meet
    With welcoming smiles his true and fond caress;
His little ones will gather round his feet,
    And humble happiness his hours will bless.
Ah! praised be God for all the garnered love
    That makes our earthly pilgrimage so bright,
Leading our thoughts to mansions fair above,
    Where never falls the darkness of the night.

WINTER.

THE tattered robes of autumn cling
  Around the trembling forest trees,
Falling at touch of wild bird's wing
  Or sighing of the troubled breeze.
The gorgeous beauty of her prime
  Has faded from the woods away ;
A stranger from an arctic clime
  Woos the sad earth by night and day

He hangs her brow with jewels rare,
  He wraps her form in ermine white,
And gems a queen might deign to wear
  Gleam, from its folds, prismatic light.
In vain is all the wealth he brings ;
  She sadly sighs for days agone,
For autumn's bright and beauteous things,
  For summer's laughing, joyous tone.

At his embrace her heart grows chill;
  She shudders as he clasps her round;
The pulses of her life stand still,
  A bride reluctant he has found.
Alas! she mourneth not alone
  The hours that are for ever past,
The happy days for ever flown,
  Too brightly beautiful to last.

I know of eyes now dim with tears,
  I know of breasts grown strangely cold,
For wintry smiles and questioning fears
  Have changed those loving eyes of old.
Oh, would that Summer in the heart
  Might ever hold her gentle reign,
Or if stern Winter claims a part
  She would resume her sway again.

But no. Unlike the changing years,
  When once her radiant form has flown
In vain you woo her smiles or tears,
  In vain the living dead you mourn.
Ah! cherish, then, your summer days,
  Your autumn glories, as they fly;
Too soon will come the wintry rays
  When all their beauties fade and die.

O

SONNETS.

I.

MORNING.

THE morning breaks.   Across the amber sky
Grey clouds are trooping slowly one by one,
Their edges crimsoned by the rising sun.
 Mist wreaths upon the distant mountains lie,
And violet vapours through the valley glide,
  Veiling the crystal stream that winds along,
  For ever murmuring, in low, gushing song,
To the sweet flowers and fern that droop beside.
 My heart to God springs up in thankful prayer !
Most beautiful on such a morn doth seem
This earth; most radiant, as the sun's first gleam
  Flashes afar athwart the woodland fair.
In pleasant ways my pilgrimage is cast :
God only grant these happy days may last!

II.

NOON.

THE glorious sun is midway in the sky,
But for the clouds it scarcely can be seen ;
Their shadows fall across the meadows green,
    And o'er the brown fields where the sheaves
    still lie.
Ah! now my heart is filled with boding dread,
    And tears break slowly from my downcast eyes
    Like drops of rain from all unwilling skies,
When April's flowers bloom fair above the dead.
    A whisper trembles through the noontide air ;
The rustling of the pines the wind before,
Mayhap, yet sounds a dirge like 'nevermore.'
    And back I gaze upon the past so fair,
Yet glean not courage for the coming night,
From whence I see no ray of guiding light !

III.

NIGHT.

TO-NIGHT a thick mist fills the valley wide,
And banks of clouds wall in the arching skies,
Hiding the starlight from my wistful eyes.
  Black loom the rocks upon the dark hill-side,
And all is drear and lone, where late, so gay,
  The reapers toiled amid the golden grain,
  Leaving the ripened field with loaded wain,
To wait the dawning of another day.
  O gloomy night! thy shadows fall on me,
As in the shrouded future I divine
Still darker hours than ever yet were mine.
  Then o'er my breast the waves of sorrow's sea
Shall beat more fiercely for the calm before.
Ah, Life! how wild the storms that sweep thy
    shore!

ERAS IN LIFE.

FOREBODINGS.

'An imminence of something unknown is felt.'
'Forebodings come, we know not how or whence,
Shadowing a nameless fear upon the soul.'—MISS PROCTER.

WHAT weight is this which presses on my soul ?
　　Powerless to rise, I sink upon the dust ;
The days in solemn cycle o'er me roll,
　　While, praying, I can only wait and trust ;

Trust the dear Hand that all my life has led
　　Through pastures green, by waters pure and still ;
If now He leads me through dark ways, and
　　　　dread,
　　Shall I dare murmur, whatso'er His will ?

Give me, dear Lord, the strength I so much
　　　　need—
　　Do Thou but guide through earth-defiling ways,
Then will I follow where Thy hand doth lead,
　　With feet unfaltering in my darkest days.

December 1872.

THORNS AND ARROWS.

ONE day I made complaint because some thorns
Had pierced me when I stooped to find a flower,
Forgetting no rose bloomed without such dower
Down the long years of fair and dewy morns.

Another time I wept some bitter tears
In that from pleasant pastures I had strayed,
While in a labyrinth my way was laid,
Which seemed as endless as the untold years.

Once more I made lament ; and that was when
A creature, bright with many-coloured hues,
Which fearful I the thing its life would lose
Had rescued from the slime of bog and fen,

In which it struggling lay, and gasped for breath ;
And when in safety on my hearth 'twas laid,
I fed it from my hand, nor felt afraid
That it would turn and sting me to my death.

But all in vain my simple trust had birth :
The creature struck its fangs against my heart ;
Save that it found no vulnerable part,
I now would be but as a clod of earth.

There came an hour in which I made no moan,
But sat apart from morn to eve, nor wept,
And through long laggard nights my watch I
    kept,
With heart more heavy than the quarried stone.

Then said I, 'Sage and seer are true who write
That little troubles most our lives will fret,
And pierce the heart with poison-fanged regret,
And loudest make lament by day and night.

'But when some mortal anguish smites its blow,
The sore heart hides its pain from searching eyes,
Stifles each moan and checks the telltale sighs
That would reveal the torture of its woe.'

And then I prayed : 'O God, for ever just !
Forgive me that I made such loud complaint
O'er ills that every human life must taint,
Till the immortal rends its robe of dust.

'But now, dear Lord, Thou knowest all my grief,
Thou seest how my heart is drenched in blood,
And how my tears surge in a prisoned flood
That, pent within my breast, brings no relief.

' Canst Thou not draw the arrow from my heart
And stay the bleeding ere my life flows out?'
Why should I ask or let one wretched doubt
Within my questioning soul have place or part?

He sees my woe, He knows its bitter cause;
He weighs my heart, He counts my prisoned tears
And all my dead hopes shrouded on their biers;
And when His time arrives, He will not pause,

But draw the arrow if its work be o'er,
And close the wound until it leaves no scar,
And raise the dead from sepulchres ajar,
And, born anew, my hopes and joys restore.

MY GETHSEMANE.

ALL night I wept and prayed, and prayed and
   wept,
But when the morning came the pain was there;
I could not drown my sorrow with my tears,
   Nor could I lose it in long hours of prayer.
Then to my memory came a holy spot
   Where once I knelt in a far eastern land,—
The cave where Christ withdrew within the mount,
   Leaving in sleep's soft arms his cherished band.
The votive lamps burned low before the shrine,
   Where flowers heaped in loving offerings lay,
And costly incense heavy made the air,
   While pilgrims knelt from morn till eve to pray.
Here had my Saviour wrestled with His soul,
   While drops like blood streamed down His pallid
      face;
Here had the angel ministered to Him:
   Here had His heart been filled with heavenly
      grace.

But not from Him the bitter cup did pass :
  An angel held it while He drank its lees.
Dear God, must I too drain this bitter cup,
  In my Gethsemane, on bended knees ?
Ah ! here I'll wait Thy angel, for I know
  No soul is left to struggle on alone :
Sooner or later comes the strength we ask,
  Sooner or later are our sorrows flown.

'O GOD, BE PITIFUL!'

TEMPTATION TO DOUBT GOD'S PROVIDENCE AND RESISTANCE
TO HIS WILL.

AGAINST a wall of rock my helpless hands
Beat with the fierceness of despairing force ;
The darkness settles round, and not one ray
Pierces the deadly gloom where late the sun
Sprinkled its light and warmth in golden showers.
I thought the earth so grandly beautiful,
The universe but made for sweetest joys,
And now where is the beauty, where the joy ?
I fold my weak, bruised hands across my heart,
And from its depths my soul sends forth the cry,
'O God, be pitiful!' And still the rocks
Loom high, and still the darkness ever grows,
And neither God nor man is pitiful.

What knowest thou of God, complaining soul,
That thou shouldst dare to doubt His pitying love ?

P

If, wandering from the paths in which thy feet
Were set, thou strayest into darkness blank
And fall against the rocks that keep us well
Within their bounds, rather give thanks to Him
Who stretched the barrier for our good, to save
Our feet from farther straying.   God not pitiful!
Recall the impious thought, and ne'er forget
That no soul cries in vain, ' Be pitiful, O God !'

'*BE BRAVE!*'

BE brave! poor heart, be brave!
And suffer and grow strong!
Just when the night the darkest is
The day will break ere long.

Be brave! sad heart, be brave!
And falter not nor fear:
For when the road the longest seems
The turning-point is near!

Be brave! strong heart, be brave!
These words say o'er and o'er,
Until the heart has ceased to beat,
And lips can plead no more!

SUBMISSION.

I KNEW not Thou didst close and seal
  The fountains in my pilgrim life—
That I should traverse arid plains,
  Encountering Bedouin strife.

I knew not it was Thou, or else
  I would not so have murmured, Lord,
To find my gushing fountains sealed,
  My palm-trees fallen on the sward.

I knew not whence the arrows flew
  That tore my bleeding heart in twain ;
For had I known Thine was the mark,
  I could have borne the torturing pain.

I knew not that Thy guiding love
  Decreed from idols, I had made,
I must be torn to do Thy will :
  And knowing not, I was afraid.

But now I see that it is Thou,
  Welcome the loss, the pain, the strife ;
For whatsoever is Thy will
  Shall always be my will in life.

EVIL AND GOOD.

'The soul of good in things evil.'—STOPFORD BROOKE.

'A sublime feeling of a presence comes about me at times.'

F. W. ROBERTSON.

IN the lap of the mountains I lie,
Looking up to the cloudland of sky,
While a vision, keen, piercing, and clear,
Descends from the gods to me here,
Till I see the pale spirits troop by.

What mission have they to fulfil?
And is it of good or of ill?
No answer from far or from near;
And trustful I rest without fear,
And wait as before on God's will.

I hear not a breath nor a sigh,
Yet some power for ever is nigh:
Some Presence beside me keeps guard,
Around me to watch and to ward,
And evil for ever must fly.

Yet evil clings close to the good,
As the rough bark clings to the wood;
And evil its course must perform
Through sorrow and darkness and storm,
Through fire of trial withstood.

And good with the evil must grow:
In the field where white lilies blow
Bloom the blood-red blossoms of sin:
We know not how deeply within
Strikes their stain on bosoms of snow.

But the stain, the sin and the pain,
And the grief, is never in vain:
We suffer, endure, and grow strong,
And our right is born of our wrong;
And through fire our gold we regain!

SAN MORITZ: *August* 1879.

WRECKED.

WEIRD was the face of the ocean,
  Wild was the pitiless blast,
As driven before it madly
  A vessel's wreck swept past.

Out of the gaping port-holes
  Poured seas of foaming brine ;
From battered hulk to broken masts
  No living thing made sign.

Straightway in dreams before me
  My own wrecked life passed by—
When I was left on seas of grief
  To sink with no help nigh.

But He who holds the ocean
  In hollow of His hand
Guided that vessel into port
  And brought me to the land.

The stanch ship, stored with treasure
　Of silver and of gold,
Held all confided to its care
　Safe in its iron hold.

My barque, though wrecked, deserted,
　Holds now its treasure still,
And He who brought it into port
　Does with it as He will.

DEAD HOPES.

I HAVE left my life behind me,
I have buried my past to-day,
And turned the lock of the grave-yard
  And given the key away.

I know will come days of longing—
O days of unspeakable dread !—
When I shall go back in spirit
  To look on my precious dead.

But I shall not faint nor falter,
Nor show by a word nor a sign,
How I mourn for what lies buried
  In this grave-yard heart of mine.

And they who know not my anguish,
My woe, and its deathless pain,
Will smile with kind words of greeting,
  Counting my loss as my gain.

Their smiles with smiles I will answer,
For they shall not read in my face
How I mourn my dead hopes buried,
    How I watch the sacred place.

Whate'er befalls in the future,
Life's lessons have taught me to say,—
' The Lord directeth the steps of man,
    Though his heart devise the way.'

WAITING.

OVER the sea, over the sea, eyes of mine look
    wistfully :
Day follows night, and night follows day,
And night and day are one alway,
As over the sea, over the sea, eyes of mine look
    wistfully.

Over the sea, over the sea, eyes of mine look
    earnestly :
I see no isle, I see no shore,
I only hear the billows roar,
As over the sea, over the sea, eyes of mine look
    earnestly.

Over the sea, over the sea, eyes of mine look
    dreamily :
I soon will hear the pilot's call,
With sound of oars that rise and fall,
As over the sea, over the sea, eyes of mine look
    dreamily.

Over the sea, over the sea, eyes of mine look
    fearlessly :
The pilot Death is near at hand,
He steers his bark unto this strand,
As over the sea, over the sea, eyes of mine look
    fearlessly.

Over the sea, over the sea, eyes of mine look
    eagerly :
I see the gold and jasper gate,
I see the angels watch and wait,
As over the sea, over the sea, eyes of mine look
    eagerly.

Over the sea, over the sea, eyes of mine look
    tenderly :
I see the faces gone before
Watching for me at heaven's door ;
Over the sea, over the sea, take me, pilot, tenderly !

MEMORIAL.

' OH, tell me, are the fields of heaven
  As fair as earth's are now,
With all their wealth of living green
  And roseate bloom of bough ?

' I think when frosts of autumn come
  And leaves grow brown and sere,
The fading of the flowers would make
  E'en heaven more fair appear.'

The autumn came, with gorgeous wealth
  Of opalescent glow ;
She faded with the fading leaf,
  Before the winter's snow.

The spring's soft green, the summer's bloom,
  The autumn's drifts of gold,
Are now as nought to one who walks
  In fairer scenes untold.

But they who loved her miss her most
　When spring's first blossoms blow,
And when the leaves of autumn burn
　With red and golden glow.

For always doth the spring recall
　Her lingering love of earth,
And autumn brings the memory
　Of her immortal birth.

THE MINISTERING SPIRIT.

FOUR gates there are that open into heaven :
　The first of deep-hued amethyst, fold on fold ;
The second, jacinth is ; the third of pearl ;
　The fourth, of inwrought work of jewelled gold.

The amethyst gate they only enter in
　In whom both 'faith and charity' abound ;
Good works' the jacinth ; 'pure of heart' the pearl ;
　The fourth, they who were tried, nor wanting
　　found.

Weary of earth, heart-sore and faint, there came
　A pilgrim spirit to the purple gate :
Its violet folds were closed, and opened not
　To give one glimpse of heaven's celestial state.

On to the jacinth gate the traveller went:
　Its amber crystal rose like wall of glass,
Nor open swung at her imploring cry,
　Within to let the weary wanderer pass.

The gate of pearl, with prism-glowing tints,
  Feebly she next with faltering hands essayed ;
A message came : 'Pass to the golden gate !
  Our King awaits thee there. Be not afraid !'

Emboldened thus, the woman hastened on :
  The gate flew open ; throngs on either side
Welcomed with amaranth wreaths and sound of
    harps
  As forth to meet her came 'The Crucified.'

Within the jewelled gate the pilgrim passed,
  Led by her Lord, transfigured like to Him,
While wave on wave of music flowed through
    heaven
  From chanting, winged hosts of seraphim.

Amazed, the earth-born to her Saviour said,
  'What wrought I, Lord, for Thy dear name on
    earth,
That Thou shouldst meet *me* at the gate of gold—
  Accused, reviled, my good name robbed of
    worth ?'

Q

' Living for others, thou hast lived for Me ;
  Conquering thyself, the conqueror's crown is
  given :
Faithful in all committed to thy care,
  Hath brought thee through the golden gate to
  heaven.'

And now, no longer weary nor heart-sore,
  This pilgrim spirit works for mortals still ;
No longer fettered by earth's fears and cares,
  But free as angels are to do God's will.

Now, to the wayworn on this planet left,
  On viewless pinions borne, she comes and goes;
They know not whence the calm sustaining strength
  That to them ofttimes like a river flows !

Ah, messengers there are from heaven to earth,
  In these our days, as in the days of old :
And those sent back to strengthen and console
  Are they who enter by the gate of gold !

LONDON : PRINTED BY
SPOTTISWOODE AND CO., NEW-STREET SQUARE
AND PARLIAMENT STREET